SUN, SEA AND MURDER

An Inspector Alvarez Mystery

Roderic Jeffries

This first world edition published 2009
in Great Britain and in the USA by
SEVERN HOUSE PUBLISHERS LTD of
9–15 High Street, Sutton, Surrey, England, SM1 1DF.
Trade paperback edition published
in Great Britain and the USA 2009 by
SEVERN HOUSE PUBLISHERS LTD

British Library Cataloguing in Publication Data

Jeffries, Roderic, 1926-
  Sun, sea and murder. - (An Inspector Alvarez mystery)
  1. Alvarez, Enrique (Fictitious character) - Fiction
  2. Police - Spain - Majorca - Fiction 3. Hit-and-run
  drivers - Fiction 4. Detective and mystery stories
  I. Title
  823.9'14[F]

  ISBN-13: 978-0-7278-6747-6   (cased)
  ISBN-13: 978-1-84751-107-2   (trade paper)

Typeset by Palimpsest Book Production Ltd.,
Grangemouth, Stirlingshire, Scotland.
Printed and bound in Great Britain by
MPG Books Ltd., Bodmin, Cornwall.

ONE

The car twitched on the wet road before the traction control killed the potential skid. Tyler told himself he must drive more slowly. It had been a good lunch; a very good lunch. The wine – Clos de . . . Clos de something, had surpassed its reputation; the cognac, Courvoisier Wellington . . . Napoleon? He must remember to tell Bill that and hear the deep belly laugh. A good cognac was captured sunshine. He found he was heading towards the grass verge and hurriedly altered course.

A triangular field ready to be harvested marked the beginning of his estate. He chuckled.

He passed Fiddler's Wood. Who was Fiddler? A corruption of the local word 'fibbler' meaning thief. Some old fool had recently told him that it was just the name of one of the past owners of the wood. No Fiddler was mentioned in the estate's papers.

He looked down at the clock on the dashboard and could not immediately read the time. Then his sight sharpened. It was already five and he had told Julia he would be with her by four. She would be in a bad mood. Would shout that he never could be bothered to show her any respect. Strange how women of her ilk demanded the illusion of respect. Their shield from reality? The later he was, the longer it would take to warm her up. He increased speed and failed to note Hopfeld Corner until he was almost upon it.

He braked sharply as he turned in to the corner, but this time the car was unable to counter his stupidity. The skid took him across the road and into a man and woman who had been walking arm-in-arm along the lane. The man was thrown violently to the left, the woman up and on to the bonnet and then on to the road.

He braked to a halt. Shock cleared his mind sufficiently to understand that to stop there and call for an ambulance would lead to his being breathalysed by the police and found to be well over the limit. Then, what chance would he have of claiming the couple had suddenly stepped off the grass verge in front of the car or that the steering had failed?

His mind raced. The car had hit them with such force they must be either severely injured or dead. His wealth would count against him, thanks to the common hatred of success, and the law would pursue him with zeal. He might have to face the charge of causing death by dangerous driving when under the influence. The usual penalty for that was jail. But jail was for the robber, the rapist, the corrupt businessman, not people like he. He drove on, desperately trying to work out how to escape suspicion of guilt.

The light rain had stopped and the sky was beginning to clear. A car pulled to a stop and Detective Inspector Knox climbed out, lifted the police tape to pass under it, crossed to where Detective Sergeant Cameron stood.

'What's the latest on the victims?'

'One dead on arrival, one critically ill and unlikely to survive.'

'Shit!'

They watched the forensic team, in white plastic suits, finger-searching the road and grass verge. Knox was silent for a short while as he visually assessed the area and the searchers, then asked: 'Do we know who they were?'

'Neither of them carried any ID. They're likely locals since they had been walking and judging by the lack of coats, before the brief drizzle stated. I've sent a Uniform along to see if he can learn anything in Eastingford which is the next village, half a mile or so further on.

'The chap from Vehicles is reasonably certain the car was driving down that lane' – he pointed – 'came in to the corner far too quickly, went into a skid which took him into the couple. So far, Forensics have found a broken wing mirror very recently wrenched off its stand, so there's good reason to think it was from the crash car. Seems likely the mirror's from a luxury job.'

Knox brought a pack of cigarettes from his pocket. 'Smoke?'

'Not for the past couple of years, sir.'

'Want to live long enough to draw your pension?' The two men liked and respected each other; their relationship was as near friendship as rank allowed. Knox lit a cigarette. 'Let's hear your thoughts.'

'These lanes don't lead directly to anywhere and become a bit of a maze if you don't know your way around, so the driver might well be local.'

'Or visiting friends who live nearby. Whichever, he will have driven off as if the hounds of hell were gnawing at the back tyres, assuming the driver was a man. Can't see a woman carrying on, careless of what happened to the couple. If he's fairly local, he'll have reached home some time ago. If he's not local, he'll have made for the quickest possible escape route. How far is the nearest motorway junction?'

'A couple of miles.'

'Are there speed cameras there?'

'Can't say, Guv. I'll get on to Traffic and find out.'

'Tell them we're looking for a car, luxury class, which has lost a wing mirror and is being driven at high speed.'

The victims were identified on Sunday. Irene Drew, twenty-one. Blaise Newcome, twenty-six. Partners for a couple of years and intending to marry in August.

It was Knox's task to inform the parents of the tragic deaths. A task he hated and which left him emotionally disturbed for a long time.

Traffic had reported that cameras on the motorway had recorded a car heading south at speeds ranging from 90 to 115 miles an hour. It was identified as a Bentley and its nearside wing mirror was missing. Registered in the name of Tyler, Two Oaks Manor.

'Something in this case is out of kilter,' Knox said suddenly as they drove out of the town of Arlington and entered countryside.

'Why so?' Cameron asked as he changed gear.

'The car's registered in the name of a local estate owner. If he was driving, why head for the motorway instead of home; hoping we'd fail to trace the car and he could hide it until it would be safe to have it repaired without comment?'

'Sheer panic?'

'Wouldn't that rush him to the supposed security of home?'

'Maybe the driver was one of the staff, too terrified to go back and report what had happened.'

Knox stared out at a field in which a herd of Friesians were strip grazing. 'Have you ever wanted to live in the country?'

'I wouldn't mind it, but Gwen certainly would.'

'Why so?'

'She'd feel cut-off, too lonely.'

'A degree of solitude, yes, but in this day and age that's a luxury. Win enough money and it'll be an Elizabethan farmhouse for the wife and me; oak beams, inglenook fire-places, and a shoe bricked up in the wall.'

'A what?'

'When they built a house in those days, they bricked up a shoe to bring good luck to everyone who lived in it. I could do with a life in which there's more good luck than bad.'

'The only way you'll find that is to retire from the force.'

'True.'

They turned right and drove past a small wood, a part of which had recently been cut down.

'You don't see that very often these days,' Knox remarked.

'See what, Guv?'

'Coppicing.'

'So what's that when it's at home?'

'No one will ever mistake you for a countryman.'

'Because I sometimes smile?'

A cock pheasant suddenly flew out of the hedgerow and with frantically beating wings, voiding, flew across the front of the car.

'Another ten miles an hour and I could have had it for supper,' Cameron said.

'A poacher who's totally ignorant of the countryside?'

'That would be a gift, not a poach . . . We're just about there. In ten minutes, we'll know if the butler did it.'

Weak humour helped to counter emotions.

They drove through the stone gateway, with elaborate wrought-iron gates, and up the curving drive which was lined with rhododendron bushes. Two Oaks Manor was misnamed. The two oaks, once locally renowned for their age and girth, had been felled at the beginning of the last century, and the oblong Edwardian building could hardly have looked less like a traditional manor house.

They left the car, crossed the gravel and stepped into the elaborate portico. On the heavy, panelled door was a fox's head with a ring through its mouth.

'Reminds me of a film I saw when I was a kid,' Cameron said. 'Scared the daylights out of me because when the door opened, a werewolf stood there.'

'Can we pass over your childhood excesses and move on?'

Cameron lifted the heavy ring and knocked twice.

The door was opened by a nearly-middle-aged woman who wore an apron over her dress and carried an old-fashioned duster in her right hand.

'Detective Inspector Knox and Detective Sergeant Cameron,' Knox said.

She looked uncertainly at him.

Knox spoke pleasantly. 'We've come to talk to Mr Tyler. Is he here?'

She shook her head.

'Then we'd better have a word with you. May we come in?'

She hesitated, finally said: 'I suppose it'll be all right.'

They entered a hall, unexpectedly small considering the size of the house. On two of the walls hung pompous paintings, one of an elderly man, the other an elderly woman. She led the way into the sitting room, which was luxuriously furnished yet lacked any touch of family life. They settled on comfortable armchairs.

'For a start,' Knox said with light humour, 'we'd better know who you are?'

'Mrs Peterson. I'm the housekeeper and my husband is the gardener.' She spoke uneasily.

'And between you, you obviously keep everything in apple-pie order.'

She did not respond to the laboured flattery.

'Like I said, we wish to have a word with Mr Tyler to find out if he can help us.'

'Then he's not in any trouble?'

'Would that be likely?'

'But why . . .?' She did not finish.

'Maybe you can tell us where he is right now?'

'I can't.'

'So when did you last see him?'

'When he left here yesterday to have lunch with his friends.'

'And he didn't return?'

'The husband and me were out since it was our afternoon and evening off.'

'Then you assumed he'd returned before you did?'

'That's right. So when it was time this morning, I phoned up to see what he wanted for breakfast and there was no answer.'

'What did you think had happened?'

'Couldn't tell. Never says what he's going to do. Only I told the husband to go up and see if he was in bed and not very well. Goes up and knocks; there's no answer, so he opens the door and calls out. Don't like to walk straight in. Sometimes has a friend staying.'

'Female?'

She sniffed.

'Was someone with him?'

'The husband came back down and said the bed hadn't been slept in.'

'Did that surprise you?'

'Not really.'

'So, his car was in the garage?'

'Only the small one was there.'

'He has a large one as well?'

'Course he does,' she answered with surprise.

'What make is the large car?'

'A Bentley. Why d'you want to know?'

'Idle curiosity, Mrs Peterson. It's interesting to know how other people live. You said that yesterday he had lunch with friends. Do you know their names?'

'Mr and Mrs Dell.'

'Have you phoned them to find out if he stayed with them for the night?'

'He wouldn't like me doing that. Think I was snooping on his life.'

'Nevertheless, would you ask them now?'

She left the room, soon returned. 'He left them late in the afternoon.'

'Will you give me their telephone number? It may be necessary to have a word with them.'

She turned back towards the door.

'At the same time, will you find a photograph of him?'

The question worried her further, but she left without comment. When she returned, she handed him a square of paper on which was a phone number and a photograph of a man in riding kit seated on a horse.

'Thanks,' Knox said. He stood. 'We'll leave you in peace ... Oh! there is one other question. Does Mr Tyler own a property abroad?'

'Yes.'

'Do you know where?'

'On the island.'

'Which island would that be?'

'Majorca.'

'Lucky man. Sun, sea, sangria and—' He stopped abruptly. 'Whereabouts in Majorca?'

'Port something.'

'Have you any suggestions as to what the something might be?'

'Can't rightly remember.'

'Perhaps you'd look through his address book and anything else to see if you can find the name and address of the house?'

'Can't do that.'

'Why?'

'Because I don't go looking through people's personal things,' she said sharply.

'Very understandable. If you should recall the address, let me know, will you?' Knox handed her a card. 'That's the phone number and if you ask for me, they'll put you straight through.'

Seven minutes later, they drove out of the grounds on to the road.

'Did you notice the old girl's expression when you suggested she searched through his stuff for the address?' Cameron asked.

'Nice to meet such honesty – except in a case like this.'

'You'll ask for a search warrant?'

'On the grounds we have right now, no magistrate would think twice before lecturing me on the requirements for a successful application.'

'Then . . . are you thinking what I'm thinking?'

'It's to be hoped not,' Knox answered ironically.

'Tyler realized his only hope of escaping arrest was to get the car out of the country so all the damage from the collision could be repaired before there was any reasonable chance of our finding it. Without the physical proof the damaged car could provide, all he could be charged with would be driving too quickly on the motorway.'

'So you visit the Dells and tactfully find out how much Tyler had to drink at lunch. You then request a visual search of all CCTV videos covering the Euro Tunnel and the ferries from five thirty onwards on Saturday.'

TWO

Alvarez, sitting at the table in the sitting-cum-dining room, dunked a piece of *ensaïmada* in hot chocolate.

'You realize what the time is?' Dolores called out from the kitchen.

He looked at his watch, and was vaguely surprised to note it was already twenty-five past eight.

'If you don't hurry up, you won't arrive at the post before it's time to return for lunch.'

He pulled off another piece of *ensaïmada*. 'What's for lunch?'

'I'm far too busy to worry about that now.'

'Perhaps *Estafado de buey*?' he suggested hopefully. When she cooked a pot roast of beef, carrots, turnips, bacon, onions, garlic and spices, in red wine, it was a dish in the gastronomic premier league.

'As my mother used to say, "A woman works while a man dreams."'

Not for the first time, he wondered why her mother had so often expressed contempt for men. Her husband should have corrected her very early in their marriage.

She stepped through the bead curtain across the kitchen doorway. 'You do not intend to work today?'

'There's no rush.'

'Not for you, since you are incapable of rushing. But for me, having to look after a family and my tired cousin, I cannot enjoy the luxury of rest. I need to clear and polish the table, so you will move.'

He picked up plate and mug, crossed to the nearest chair, sat.

'Should I have apologized for not waiting until it was convenient for you to move out of the way?'

He ate the last piece of *ensaïmada*. Carlos Dolivellas had written that woman was an enigma of unpredictability. Perhaps he had known a Dolores who spoke with a sharpened tongue. A pity a woman's character was not more like a man's.

The Guardia Civil post was a reasonably short walk away. He might have considered undertaking it had not the day already been so burning hot. When a man sweated, he lost necessary salts. One should not risk the body's suffering such deprivation. He drove to work.

The duty cabo congratulated him on arriving at work so early; he ignored the puerile comment, crossed to the stairs and climbed them, not pausing to regain his breath until out of sight of the cabo. Once seated in his office, he toyed with the idea of eating, smoking and drinking less, as his doctor kept demanding.

Four letters had been left on his desk. He regarded them with dislike and did not open them since they would contain unnecessary information or, in the case of the envelope with the insignia of the superior chief's office, trouble.

The phone rang. He waited for it to stop, which it eventually did. He settled back in the chair and thought about the suggestions now being made on how to teach youngsters to drink sensibly. Typical political stupidity. Didn't they understand that to learn to drink sensibly, one first had to drink stupidly?

The phone rang again and he accepted it would be an idea to answer it.

'Inspector Alvarez?'

The speaker did not identify herself, but there was no need to do so. Only Salas's secretary spoke with such arrogant female superiority. 'Yes, señorita.'

'The superior chief will speak to you.'

He waited, wondering what he had done and should not have; what he had not done and should have.

'Where the hell are you?' Salas finally demanded.

'In my office in Llueso, señor.'

'I would hardly expect you to be on the top of Puig Major.'

'But you asked where was I . . .'

'And received an idiotic answer.'

'I wouldn't have said it was.'

'You are a poor judge of what you say.'

'Your secretary said you wanted to speak to me . . .'

'It would have been more accurate had she said that I unfortunately *needed* to speak to you.'

'And so I expected there to be a pause.'

'Why?'

'Either the receiver is handed over or the call is routed through. Then the person speaks.'

'You fail to understand that is what I expected?'

'I mean at the other end.'

'The other end to what?'

'The person who is listening.'

'Thus ensuring there is silence.'

'Not if the person at the other end speaks.'

'I had lunch the other day with a noted psychiatrist. Thinking he might be interested, I described your inability to speak coherently on any subject without introducing totally irrelevant and confusing circumstances. He wondered if you were suffering from some hitherto unknown mental problem. I expressed the likelihood that you were.'

There was a silence. When it became prolonged, Alvarez said: 'Are you there, señor?'

'If you are trying to be amusing, you are confusing humour with insolence. What do you have to report?'

'In respect of what, señor?'

'My orders.'

'Which ones?'

'They have not been delivered?'

He looked across at the unopened letters and again noted the one from the superior chief's office. 'Perhaps it has been delayed.'

'If you have not received it, that is obvious.'

'Should it have reached me by now?'

'Would I expect you to know what I have written if it

should not have done so? When it reaches you, you will carry out my orders immediately and with very much more energy than you normally display.'

'They concern what, señor?'

'Homicide.'

'In my area? But there's been no report . . .'

'In England.'

'Then surely that hardly concerns us here?'

'I doubt anything concerns you.' The line went dead.

As he replaced the receiver, Alvarez considered his earlier stupidity in telling Dolores he wasn't in a rush, indicating he had little work in hand. The man who looked at a pregnant ewe and mentally added a lamb to his flock would inevitably suffer a stillborn. He picked up the offending envelope, opened it, brought out two sheets of computer-printed orders.

The first paragraph was written in magniloquent terms. The request for the following enquiries to be carried out had been received from the English police. *Every inspector will understand that his investigation is to be carried out with the greatest dedication. The noble traditions of the Cuerpo must be maintained so that the English could appreciate the enviable skill of those who served in this unequalled force . . .*

He skipped a few lines before reading to the end.

He stared across his desk at nothing. Two young people whose lives had been brutally ended. Gather happiness while you can, cruel death is there a-waiting. Shadows clouded his mind as he remembered the day he had been told Juana-María had been killed by a drunken Frenchman driving wildly . . .

He reached down to the bottom right-hand drawer of the desk and brought out a glass and a half-full bottle of Soberano. Brandy quietened the sorrows of life.

About to pour himself a second comforting drink, he realized it was time for his *merienda*. He returned bottle and glass to the drawer, made his way downstairs, out on to the narrow road, along to the old square thronged with tourists, and across to Club Llueso.

Roca, the bartender, had poured out a brandy by the time he reached the bar. Roca put the glass down in front of him. 'Your expression tells me you are your usual mournful self.'

'Suppose you get me a coffee.'

'It's strange how Mallorquins seem unable to say please.'

'Wouldn't make the service any better when you're providing it.'

'So what's your problem this time? Some woman walked out on you?'

'You imagine I've time for women with all the work I have to do?'

'I'd put it the other way round. Do I think you have time for work with so many women to please?'

'Would you like me to make the coffee?'

'And forgo the pleasure of serving the magnificent Don Enrique?' Roca turned and crossed to the espresso machine.

Alvarez drank, replaced the empty glass on the bar as Roca brought him a *café cortado*. 'Make the next coñac a full measure.'

'There's not a glass big enough to hold your idea of a full measure.'

He lit a cigarette after promising himself it would be his last that morning. Roca had sarcastically commented on his gloomy mood. But how could a man be cheerful when ordered to find Cyril Tyler, whom it was believed had killed two pedestrians? He might be staying in a property he owned which was in or near to a port. Which of the dozens of ports, large and small? Not known. What did 'near' mean? Not known. The prospect was of unending work and failure.

Roca handed him a refilled glass.

'I really need that,' Alvarez said.

'Your liver doesn't.'

Back in his office, the thought of the monumental task of establishing whether a Cyril Leo Tyler owned property in the area so concerned him that it was some time before he accepted there might be a simple solution to the problem. He picked the telephone directory off the floor, turned to the Llueso section, looked through the names. It was typical of the life he suffered that there should be two C. Tylers listed.

The urbanizacíon lay at the back of Port Llueso, a kilo-metre from the sea. On both flat land and the lower slopes of a hill, the chalets, villas and apartments were, except in the dictionary of an estate agent, modest in size and quality. Alvarez turned in to a side road along which were two completed houses and one under construction. Behind and beyond them was open land, covered with *garriga* – the Mediterranean bush of broom, heather, lavender, rosemary, rock roses, irises, gladioli, wild orchids, pine and wild olive trees. A large notice in Spanish, English, German and French announced that building plots were for sale. Fifty years before, one could have bought the whole area for a handful of pesetas; now one needed countless euros to purchase a single plot.

He braked to a stop in front of a small villa of formless design with a colourful garden. The garage doors were open and inside was a Seat with Spanish plates.

He walked up the gravel path, rang the bell to the side of the plain wooden door. He heard a woman call out, then a man spoke as he opened the door. 'You're early . . .' He stopped as he faced Alvarez. 'I thought you were . . .' He switched to kitchen Spanish, soon came to a stumbling halt.

'You are Señor Cyril Tyler?' Alvarez asked in English.

'Yes.'

'I am Inspector Alvarez, Cuerpo General de Policia.'

Tyler's expression became one of nervous uncertainty.

'Who is it?' a woman called out.

'Someone from the police.'

She hurried into the pocket-sized hall. 'What's the trouble?'

'I don't know.'

'Does he speak English?'

'Yes.'

'Then haven't you asked him what he wants?'

'Not yet,'

She spoke to Alvarez. 'What is it?'

She had the look as well as the manner of a sour, forceful woman.

'I should like to ask the señor some questions.'

'We are expecting friends.'

'You are Señora Tyler?'

'Of course I am,' she answered sharply. Her husband would never be given the chance of a little amusement.'We're not free this morning, so you'll have to come back some other time.'

'Libby,' her husband said nervously, 'don't you think—'

'I am not going to have my coffee morning ruined.'

'Señora,' Alvarez said, 'I must ask your husband certain questions.'

'I said, some other time.'

'Now, señora, unless he would prefer to answer them at the Guardia post.'

'Are you trying to threaten us? Don't you understand, we are British.'

'No one could doubt that, señora.'

'Libby,' Tyler said urgently, 'you mustn't . . . Let me tell him what he wishes to know. I'm sure he'll be as quick as he can be, knowing you have guests coming.'

'And what if they arrive to find he's still here? Mabel will rush around telling everyone we're in some sort of criminal trouble.'

'If we go into the sitting room . . .'

'I receive in there. Have him in the kitchen . . . Not a good idea. I have to make the coffee and prepare the petit fours and Anne always comes into the kitchen to look around and see what she can sweetly criticize. Still, maybe the only thing to do is for me to have everyone in the kitchen and to say you're talking to a man who's advising on redecorating.'

Tyler said hurriedly: 'Please come in, Inspector.'

The sitting room was furnished in flat-pack style, the only extravagance a large television set.

'I don't want you smoking in here,' she said to Alvarez.

'I will remember that, señora.'

The door bell rang. She hurriedly left the room.

'That will be our friends,' Tyler said. 'Her friends, rather.
I hope you didn't think she was a little . . . little sharp?'

'Not at all,' Alvarez answered diplomatically.

'I was afraid . . .' There were the sounds of voices, the
clatter of high heels on a tiled floor.

'I hope . . .' Tyler began, stopped. He tried again. 'I hope
I haven't done anything wrong?'

'I am here to confirm you haven't, señor.'

The answer confused Tyler.

'Do you live here or do you come on holidays?'

'We live here all the time.'

'Do you own a house in England?'

'We sold it in order to come out here. I . . . Frankly, I did
wonder at the time if it was a sensible thing to do. I mean,
everything is so different. But a couple of the wife's friends
had come out and said it was perfect. Funny thing is, the
friends returned home soon after we arrived. But we now
like it very much,' he added, and sounded less than honest.

'When were you last in England?'

'Haven't been for a couple of years. The wife was back
last year but I didn't go. She was staying with her brother
and him and me don't see things the same way.'

'Relationships often unfortunately become difficult. Do
you own a car?'

'Wouldn't want to be without one. It's not all that far
to the shops, but she likes to go every day and on to the
beach and my old bones don't like walking as they
used to.'

'Is that your Seat in the garage?'

'Yes. Why?'

'You bought it on the island?'

'That's right.'

'How long ago?'

'Must be three years . . . You haven't said why you want
to know all that.'

'I am trying to identify someone who may have witnessed
a fatal road accident in England and there was the possibility it might have been you.'

Tyler said hurriedly: 'Like I said, I haven't been back for ages. When I was there, I never saw any accident.'

'Señor, I am satisfied you know nothing about it. The only reason I had for questioning you was the person who might have seen this accident has the same name as you.'

'You mean, Cyril *Leo* Tyler?'

'I cannot yet say. Do you know him?'

'Yes.' After a pause, he added: 'But if you asked him if he knew me, he'd say he didn't.'

'Why should that be?'

'He doesn't get friendly with people like the wife and me. He's a snob, if you know what that means?'

'I have had cause to understand, more than once.'

'Soon after we moved here, we were invited to the same party as him. The wife . . . she thought it would be nice to meet someone we'd heard a lot about. I tried to get a conversation going by mentioning we had the same initial Christian and surnames. He said, "Really?" and walked away. I was blamed for being socially inept, but he'd have reacted like that whatever I said.'

It was easy to visualize the scene. Cyril Tyler diffidently trying to strike an acquaintance with someone scornful of lesser tribes. 'Presumably, he is wealthy?'

'Got more money than manners, that's for certain.'

'Is he on the island now?'

'So someone said. I wouldn't know.'

'I understand he lives up Val de Teneres.'

'If that's what it's called. We went to look at his place. An old *possessío*. Big enough to house an army.'

'Perhaps he has a large house in England as well?'

'Betty, who knows him well – too well according to some . . . Shouldn't have said that. If the wife ever hears . . .'

'She will not do so from me. Your friend Betty has been to his house in England?'

'So she says often enough. He owns an estate. Easy to imagine him strutting around, entertaining local nobs, shooting pheasants. The English country gentleman.'

Alvarez stood. 'You have helped me, señor, for which my thanks. I don't expect to have to trouble you again.

Please apologize to the señora from me for disturbing her party.'

'The only thing that would disturb their chattering would be an H bomb.'

As he left the house, Alvarez looked at his watch. Val de Teneres was some way away and it would take time to reach it.

THREE

The one drawback of a siesta was that it had to end. Newly awakened, Alvarez stared up at the ceiling of his bedroom and watched the reflected sunlight, in broad beams because of the shutters, dance to the heat of the granite window sill. If he were as rich as Cyril Leo Tyler must be, there would be no need for him to get up until he wished to, no superior chief to harass him day and night, no growing body of work which should have been completed days before.

Fantasy had to give way to reality. He must arise and question Cyril Leo Tyler. Descriptions marked him as arrogantly certain; wealth raised him above the common herd, so indifferent to others that he could drive into two young people and hurl them to the ground, continue, careless of the fact that immediate medical treatment might save one or both their lives. If he were the guilty man – and there seemed little room for doubt even if there was as yet no proof – it would be more than justice to arrest him, it would be a pleasure.

As Alvarez drove along the old road of many twists and turns, his mind was more in the past than the present. Es Teneres was a possessío and in the past, when distances were measured by walking or riding, the owner of such a home and surrounding land was in some respects monarch of all he surveyed. A few such land owners arrogated further rights to themselves which the law did not recognize, but when the law was far distant and there was much poverty, these were seldom challenged. Amongst those who were still remembered for their harsh disregard for others, Santiago Garcia's name was the most reviled. None had so wantonly embraced the devil's creed. Any young woman working in the fields might attract him. Should she resist his advances, he would threaten to throw her and her family off his land, leaving them to find work elsewhere at a time when the chances of succeeding were slight. There were some who sacrificed their honour to save their families; others could not face the shame and fled with their families to face poverty, even starvation . . . The world never had been, and never would be, free of Santiago Garcias, Alvarez thought despondently.

Two-thirds of the way along the ancient road, only partially metalled, a track branched off to the north and led to the narrow, fairly short Val de Teneres. As he passed through the sloping rock walls of the entrance, Es Teneres came into sight in the middle of the valley floor.

He had first seen the manor house many years before it had been renovated and had been nearing the state at which renovation would not be financially viable . . . Whilst doing his army service, he and a companion had been detailed to set up a stand at the end of the valley to keep watch for men who were reputed to be carrying consignments of smuggled cigarettes from the beaches which lay beyond the mountains and hills. One night – a Sunday – they had heard the distant sound of mules' feet on rock and had prepared to challenge the oncomers, only to feel knives at their throats and the quietly spoken warning that if they wished to see the sun rise, they should do nothing, hear nothing, see nothing. That was their report to the sergeant. Alvarez had never managed to decide whether he had played the part of a wise man or a coward.

He braked to a halt in front of Es Teneres. He crossed the drive, climbed the two granite steps, entered the portico and rang the bell. The door was opened by a young woman, wearing an apron, whose midnight black hair framed a pleasantly featured face. 'Yes?' she asked.

'I'd like a word with Señor Tyler. Inspector Alvarez, Cuerpo.'

Her inquisitive surprise was immediate, but she merely said: 'Come on in. He's in the sitting room. I'll tell him you're here.'

The hall was large and did not offer the note of welcome that a village house's *entrada* would. The furnishings were modern, except for two leather-backed chairs, a wooden chest, heavily carved and with a massive iron lock, and a painting by a respected artist of the nineteenth century that was of a typical Mallorquin mountain scene.

She returned. 'He wants to know . . .' She stopped, stared more intently at him. 'You're Dolores's cousin.'

He failed to identify her. Many women had deep black hair, but hers was unusually luxuriant and wavy and should have spurred his memory; it didn't. If she was a relative, however distant, or a friend and Dolores learned that he had not recognized her, he would be in trouble. He tried to uncover her identity without exposing his ignorance. 'And we last met in Inca at that shop which sells and sharpens knives.'

'I don't think I've ever been there. It was at Beatriz's first communion.'

His mind clicked into gear. Julia Gustavo. Her mother was a close friend of Dolores. A lucky escape. 'Of course! I've been working so hard, my mind has become slightly muddled. Tell me, how are your parents?'

'Father was off work for a time with a bad back, but he is much better now.'

'Glad to hear that. And María?'

'She had a nasty cold and the doctor said—'

She was interrupted. Tyler stepped into the hall, addressed Alvarez sharply. 'Do you speak any English?'

'Yes, señor.'

'Then you will say what you want.' His tone was as arrogant as his words.

'I am Inspector Alvarez of the Cuerpo General. You are Señor Tyler?'

'That is not obvious? You wish to speak to me? Then you'd better come in here.' He turned in to the room behind him.

'Expects people to run when he calls,' Julia said in Mallorquin in a low voice. 'Gets furious when things don't go as he expects. If the meal's a couple of minutes late, he's shouting.'

'Impatience turns food sour in the stomach,' Alvarez observed.

'Everything has to be perfect; we even have to wear uniform when he has guests.'

'*Folie de grandeur.*'

'How's that?'

'A starling thinking it's an eagle.'

She giggled.

Tyler appeared in the doorway. 'You may speak English, but you clearly do not understand it.'

'Julia is an old friend, señor, and I have not seen her for a long time.'

'She is not paid to waste time chatting.'

'It is the habit for us to speak a few words of greeting when we meet.'

'Your definition of "few" is not mine.' He turned and entered the sitting room.

'He speaks from both ends,' Alvarez said. 'But I suppose I'd better go in and talk to him or his blood pressure will climb. Give my salutations to Jorge and María and tell them I hope we meet again soon.'

He crossed to the half-opened doorway and entered a richly furnished sitting room, cooled by the air-conditioning unit on one wall. Tyler stood to the right of a wide, open fireplace.

'Hopefully, you will now forgo any further "tradition" and tell me why you are here,' Tyler said.

The English, Alvarez thought, were past masters at expressing their conception of social differences by the tone of voice. 'There are certain enquiries I have to make, señor.'

'Which can hardly concern me.'

'I am here to determine whether or not they do.'

'I fail to understand.'

'We have been asked by the English police to find out if the driver of a car involved in a fatal incident which occurred in England is now on this island.'

Tyler failed to conceal his sense of shock before he crossed to the window and looked out.

'Two young people, a Señor Newcome and a Señorita Drew, were killed.'

'Very unfortunate, but that cannot have anything to do with me.'

'The driver's name is reported to be Tyler.'

'A common one.'

'Yet less common when his Christian name is Cyril.'

'The absurdity of that is obvious since I have been told there is another Cyril Tyler living somewhere nearby.'

'I have spoken to him and he was not the driver involved.'

'Then since I assure you neither was I, you can accept your enquiries do not concern me.' He turned around to face Alvarez. 'I am rather busy so if you would kindly now leave—'

'I have many more questions.'

'I have not the time or reason to answer them.'

'Señor, are you reluctant to be questioned about the fatal crash?'

'Of course not.'

'Then there is no reason not to discuss it.'

'Are you trying to be smart?'

'I would not attempt that.'

'I'm damned if I like your attitude.'

'Then I apologize for my manners.'

'From necessity, one becomes accustomed to the lack of them out here.' Tyler crossed to one of the chairs, sat.

'You live in England, señor?'

'Yes.'

'Whereabouts?'

'Kent.'

'And you own a farm?'

'An estate.'

'Were you there on Saturday?'

'Yes.'

'You did not leave home?'

'No.'

'You did not have lunch with friends?'

'No.'

'Might you be mixing up the days in your mind, señor?'

'No.'

'Yet your friends say you had lunch with them on Saturday.'

'What friends?'

'The English police have give the name of Jackadon.'

Tyler stood and crossed to the window again, stared out.

'You say the police are wrong or that your friends are wrong?'

'One or the other certainly is.'

'You think both have cited the wrong day yet which is the same day?'

'What the hell does it matter which day it was?'

'Because it is important. Did you have champagne before the meal?'

'Probably.'

'Did you have wine with the meal?'

'Naturally.'

'Several glassfuls?'

'You are unlikely to appreciate that when offered a fine wine, one does not swill it down, one drinks very conservatively.'

'How many glassfuls did you have?'

'How d'you expect me to remember? Two at the very most.'

'Señora Jackadon's maid thought you had four.'

'How is she supposed to know?'

'She was serving at table.'

'And when asked by some clumsy policeman, said the first thing which came into her head.'

'Did you have coñac at the end of the meal?'

'Are you going to demand how many forkfuls of rhubarb crumble I ate?'

'You can remember what the sweet was, even though you were not there?'

'I said, I mixed up the days.'

'Did you drink three coñacs?'

'One. And if that maid says anything else, she's lying.'

'Why should she do that?'

'Servants always black their employers behind their backs.'

'Was she not employed by your friends?'

'Of course she was. But her kind hate anyone they serve.'

'You are saying she was lying simply because she served you at the table?'

'Isn't that obvious? Why say I'd been drinking heavily except to make it seem—' He stopped abruptly.

'Seem what?'

'It's immaterial.'

'Perhaps you were about to say, suggest that you might have been in an unfit state to drive a car?'

'Ridiculous and insulting.'

'Did you drive home after the meal?'

'Yes.'

'You did not judge that to be unwise?'

'Why should I? I had drunk no more than at any other meal.'

'What was the time when you left your friends?'

'After six.'

'You can be certain it was that late?'

'When I say it was after six, it was.'

'The maid says it was considerably earlier.'

'I told you, she's been lying for the fun of it. I've had enough of this stupidity. You can leave.'

'The English police have given us detailed information so we could put these questions to you. But since you find my manner objectionable, would you prefer to return to England and speak to them directly?'

After a while, Tyler said: 'I apologize, Inspector. I have sounded rude. The fact is, I have been very worried because of certain financial problems and have been forced to make decisions which carry severe consequences for me if I have been wrong. So to have you come here and appear to believe, or at least consider it possible, I ran into two people and didn't call for help, just left them and drove away, is insulting, not just a mistake which can be quickly corrected. I hope you understand.'

'It is unfortunate I had to come at so stressful a moment for you, señor. But I am here, have already troubled you, so perhaps you will allow me to ask one or two more questions to satisfy the English police?'

'I'd be grateful if you could be as brief as possible.'

'Of course. When did you arrive on the island?'

'Yesterday morning.'

'How did you get here?'

'By car.'

'What kind of car do you drive?'

'A Bentley.'

'I have been asked to examine it in order to determine whether it has been in a collision.'

'The answer to that is, it has. Which is a mortifying admission since I like to think I am a good driver. I wasn't wearing sunglasses when I started to turn in to the drive and met the sun full on and for a couple of seconds was virtually blinded and ran into a bollard sited to stop people going into a drainage ditch. It stopped me very effectively.'

'Your car is here?'

'I called up the local Grua people and they put it on a low loader, took it to the garage in the port . . . You look surprised?'

'With a car of such quality . . .'

'A couple of trips back, I was strongly recommended to a local mechanic – even so, I was rather dubious about giving him my Rover which had developed a fault. He had it sorted out in no time flat. Knows his way around an engine blindfolded and when a job needs to be done quickly, he works to the finish regardless of hours and is honest enough not to find imaginary problems to shore up his bill.'

'Perhaps you are talking about Garaje Verde?'

'You obviously know the place.'

'Estában Nieto has a considerable reputation.' Partially of an unwelcome nature, Alvarez silently added. 'I do not need to trouble you any further, señor. Thank you for helping me.' He stood.

'It is to be hoped the English police understand their mistake after hearing from you.'

'I will make the facts as clear as possible.'

'Since business is now behind us, surely we can enjoy a little pleasure. Will you have a drink?'

'Thank you.'

'What would you like?'

'A coñac with just ice, please.'

Tyler left the room, returned with two glasses, one of which he handed to Alvarez. Even by Mallorquin standards, it was a large brandy and of good quality. Unlike Tyler, Alvarez thought as he drank.

FOUR

At a reasonable hour of the morning, Alvarez drove down to the port and along to Garaje Verde. It was not a garage in the conventional sense since it was the ground floor of a house and in the past where mules would have been kept. It could accommodate only the car which was being repaired; any others had to be parked outside in the road. A hole in the ground took the place of a hydraulic lift; tools and three new tyres hung on the walls; the 'office' was a desk and cupboard at the far end.

He parked, walked the twenty metres to the garage. Two men were working on the dark grey Bentley; one was down in the pit, the other was at the front end. The younger man looked up and across the bonnet. 'Enrique!'

'Didn't expect to find you here.' Emilio was the younger son of a friend.

'Dad said it was time I stopped chasing girls and started to work.'

'And you're still doing more chasing than working,' Nieto called out from the pit as he moved towards the steps.

'Work is man's curse,' Alvarez said. He visually checked that both wing mirrors were intact.

Nieto scrambled up to floor level. 'If you want something done on your car right now, you're out of luck.'

'The perfect salesman!'

'Suppose you've been driving without any oil because it's too much trouble to check the level?'

'My car's working perfectly since I don't bring it here.'

'Then why bother us?'

'I want to look at that to see whether I might buy one.' He pointed at the Bentley.

'The doors of hell will be shut and locked before you can afford that.'

Alvarez walked to the far end of the garage. There was

an inspection lamp with a long lead and he picked this up, shone it on the front end of the car. The front panels, nearside light pod and bonnet were missing. 'Been in a smash from the look of things,' he said, as he replaced the inspection lamp on the floor.

'Hit a bollard in Parelona,' Nieto said, suddenly miserly with words.

'Careless.'

'The sun blinded the owner as he was turning,' Emilio said.

'Turning where?'

'Into the drive of a friend's house.'

'Keep your breath for work,' Nieto said sharply.

'Must have been quite a thump.'

Emilio ignored Nieto's rebuke, said: 'Didn't do all that much damage.'

'When you've had to remove so much?'

'Said he wasn't going to have any dents on his car and everything needed to be as good as new and repainted.'

'Was the bonnet badly dented?'

'If it had been my car, I'd have lived with it. Pay good euros to get rid of something you couldn't really see until you got down and looked along the line of the bonnet?'

'Clear off for your *merienda*,' Nieto said angrily.

'A moment ago you were shouting at me to work.'

'Which you ain't been doing because you're so goddamn busy talking.'

'What about the wing mirror?' Alvarez asked. 'Was there one missing?'

'Does it look like there was?' Nieto asked.

'Just wondered if I was seeing double.'

'There's some think you can't see single.'

Alvarez left. He drove down to the front and parked, stared out at the bay. The far mountains edged a cloudless sky, sails of yachts and windsurfers were of many colours and design and added a touch of carnival; adults and children shouted their fun and pleasure as they played on the beach or in the sea. It was a scene to make man accept there could be joy in life.

Spiritually heartened, he walked along to the nearest front café. A drink would cost at least twice as much as in one of the back street cafés, but there were times when the soul did not want to be troubled by economy.

A waiter in open-neck white shirt, perspiring freely, came to his table.

'A coñac and a café cortado.'

As the waiter hurried away, Alvarez moved his chair further into the shade of the overhead umbrella. He looked across the pedestrianized road at a young, shapely woman in a minimal monokini lying down on her back on a towel. By her side, a man in brightly coloured shorts spoke to her and she smiled. Was he a travelling partner, a would-be holiday partner or a beach bum? The young could not understand how fortunate they were. In the past, no young woman would be unaccompanied by an elderly female relative with a suspicious mind and bikinis were forbidden by law.

The waiter brought his coffee and brandy, spiked the bill, hurried away. Alvarez read the bill and regretted his decision not to drink at a bar in a back street.

'Hullo again.'

He turned to face Emilio. 'Have you been sacked?'

'You think he could find anyone else stupid enough to accept the wages he offers? You heard him tell me to take my *merienda*.'

'At a front bar?'

'Not at any bar. In good weather, I come down and enjoy the view.'

'Of young female tourists.'

'So why are you drinking here?'

'To enjoy the natural beauty.'

'Where's the difference?'

'In an adult's mind.' It was obvious Emilio would like a drink. About to ignore that fact, Alvarez had second thoughts. Employees could sometimes provide information their bosses would not. 'Why not sit down and have a drink?'

Emilio sat, half in shade, half in sharp sunshine, which cut a line across his high forehead and tumbled hair. Alvarez

signalled to the waiter who took the order. Emilio unwrapped
a length of barra, cut in half and filled with slices of ham
and cheese.

'Estában seemed rather sharp earlier on,' Alvarez
remarked.

'He was almost cheerful until you turned up and asked
questions about the car.'

'Why should that have upset him?'

'How would I know? Are you really thinking of buying
one?'

'When I haven't robbed a bank recently? I'm following
up on a report from England. A Bentley was in an accident
and they want us to find out if the car is on the island.' He
paused. 'Bit of a coincidence, come to think of it.'

'What is?'

'Me looking for a crunched Bentley and finding one in
your outfit.'

'Cars are always hitting something.'

'Just as well, or you'd be out of a job. I suppose it was
a very solid bollard the Bentley hit?'

'Must have been. There were flakes of concrete caught
up in the metal.'

'Do you know who his friend is? The one whose bollard
he hit?'

'Never heard the name.'

The waiter brought a lager and spiked the bill.

Emilio drank. Alvarez offered him a cigarette and they
both smoked.

'You mentioned the dent on the bonnet wasn't worth
bothering about,' Alvarez remarked.

'Nor was it. But Estában was told to send it to a good
planchista who was to make certain it was perfect.'

'So where's it gone?'

'No idea. Asked Estában who he'd chosen and got an
earful for not minding my own business.'

Emilio finished his barra, emptied his glass.

'Would you like another?'

'Never say no. Bit of luck seeing you!'

'Luck for both of us.'

'How do you mean?'

'Just a thought.'

Alvarez ordered another lager and, in case the other would feel embarrassed drinking on his own, a second brandy for himself. 'Sounds as if the owner of the car is going to have a larger bill than necessary.'

'Many times larger. Take the wing mirror. Said it had to be replaced immediately. Meant having one specially brought out from Palma and it didn't matter what that cost. Since he wasn't going to be able to drive the car until all the repairs were finished, seemed daft to be in such a rush. More money than sense.'

'Better than having more sense than money.'

The waiter brought the two drinks. Alvarez slowly turned his glass between middle finger and thumb. Emilio had said far more than he had spoken. Tyler had left the scene of the accident and driven through the Continent to Barcelona where he had boarded a ferry. In Mallorca, he had had to accept he could only be safe from a charge of causing the death of the couple if all the evidence of the collision on the car had vanished. He could have taken it to the Bentley agents to have the work carried out, but they might be questioned on behalf of the English police and they would not hide anything. So! First he ran the car into something which would cause sufficient damage to cover that which had existed previously. Then he chose to take the car to Nieto, having judged him on previous visits to be a man who would respond to the offer to pay over the odds if the job was done quickly and silently. Emilio had not understood the need for verbal reticence since he had not been offered any part of the bonus.

'It must be great to be rich,' Emilio said.

'It has its drawbacks. Makes one overlook the little people.'

FIVE

Reluctantly, Alvarez lifted the receiver and dialled. 'Superior Chief Salas's office,' said his secretary in her plum-laden voice.

'I should like to speak to the superior chief, señorita.'

'Who is speaking?'

'Inspector Alvarez.'

'My work would be less onerous if you would remember to identify yourself.'

She had known who he was immediately, but needed to display the authority she believed she gained from her work.

'Yes?' said Salas with his usual curtness.

'It is Inspector Alvarez speaking, señor.'

'I have already been informed that that would be the case.'

Sometimes one had to announce oneself, sometimes one did not. 'I have a report to make.'

'Then make it.'

'I have spoken to Señor Tyler and—'

'You find it impossible to remember that a report should always identify the reason for its conception?'

'How's that?' he asked, momentarily forgetting to whom he was speaking.

'How is what?'

'I mean, I didn't quite understand you, señor.'

'Perhaps you should try to concentrate on what is being said.'

'It's just that when you spoke of conceiving a report, I thought—'

'Since for you the word "conceive" has only one meaning, you will not tell me what you thought.'

There was silence.

'Have you any intention of proceeding?'

'There are two Tylers who live in Port Llueso.'

'You will start again.'

'It is Inspector Alvarez speaking—'

'Would that there could be doubt on that score.'

'Then I don't quite understand why I'm to tell you who I am again.'

'I am equally unable to understand how you could imagine you should.'

'You told me to start again.'

'I believe I have previously mentioned I have a friend who is an eminent psychiatrist who is interested in unusual cases. I have reason to think he is beginning to consider your case is unique. I have been trying to persuade you to make your reports in the approved, logical manner. Yet you have just been repeating yourself in the unthinking manner of a parrot. Do you still not understand what it is I require?'

'I am afraid not.'

'To know why you have conducted the enquiries with which your report is related.'

'Because you ordered me to make them, señor.'

'You remind me of the words of Ricardo Vallespir. Wisdom is limited, stupidity is abundant. Your enquiries have been made as a result of what?'

'The request from England to trace whether Cyril Tyler is at present in the area and if he is, to examine his car for signs of a fatal impact.'

'We finally have a base from which to proceed. Have you succeeded in ascertaining whether the Englishman is on the island?'

'Yes. Both of him.'

'You see no numerical illogicality in your answer?'

'Unfortunately, England only provided one Christian name.'

'Why is that unfortunate?'

'Two would have saved time. I could have separated the one from the other at the beginning. That is, unless the second names were also the same. But the odds against that must be very high, you'll agree?'

'Right now, I should be grateful if I had any idea what I am being asked to agree about. Are you capable of speaking in a fathomable manner?'

'It seemed likely Tyler would have had a telephone.'

'It is unusual to find you accepting the obvious.'

'I consulted the directory and there were two C. Tylers listed. It meant I had to question both to find out which one was the one to whom I wished to speak. Cyril *Thomas* Tyler clearly was not the Tyler England is interested in. I questioned Cyril *Leo* Tyler at some length as it seemed there was good reason to do so. He owns an estate in England and a possessío here, so is very wealthy. He drives a Bentley, which is a magical car. To ride in it must be a supreme luxury; along the Croisette, it would attract the admiring attention of everyone.'

'Imaginative folly. Is it too much to hope that in between absurdities, you discovered information which has at least some bearing on the fatal collision?'

'Señor Tyler – that is Cyril *Leo* Tyler—'

'You will ignore the alternative.'

'Lives on his estate in Kent in England. He admits having visited friends for luncheon, but says it was on a different day. At the luncheon he claims to have drunk far less and to have left far later than according to the evidence we have. His car is being repaired after a collision—'

'Is there evidence of contact? Dried blood, threads of material, impact damage?'

'He claims to have driven very recently into a concrete bollard at a friend's house and the car suffered some damage to the front end.'

'It will not have occurred to you this second contact was to hide the first.'

'That was the obvious possibility.'

'Which does not mean you considered it.'

'Having spoken to Nieto—'

'Identify him.'

'He is the owner of Garaje Verde.'

'In Palma?'

'In the port.'

'You are saying that Tyler took his luxury car – described in ridiculous terms – to be repaired by some local, incompetent mechanic?'

'In fact, he is really good at his job. Like the old-time mechanics, short of learning, but long on ability. However, in my opinion, Señor Tyler did not choose him for his skill.'

'Too logical a reason for you to consider?'

'It was Nieto's ability to forget.'

'Forget what?'

'The state of the car when it was brought to him at the garage.'

'You are trying to say, in your normal, incomprehensible style, that this man will not give evidence on the original state of the car?'

'He denies there was any damage not directly attributable to the collision with the bollard. However, I later learned the truth was that the nearside wing mirror was missing and there was a slight dent on the bonnet. Tyler demanded a new mirror be fitted immediately, whatever it cost to get hold of one, even though it would be some time before the car would be fit to drive.'

'How did you gain this information?'

'Emilio told me.'

'And Emilio is who?'

'Nieto's assistant.'

'Why was he prepared to say what he did?'

'Nieto was probably reluctant to forgo any part of what he had received from Señor Tyler for his silence.'

'How typical of this island!'

'I am told, señor, that in Madrid, brown parcels are needed rather than brown envelopes.'

'To suggest bribery in Madrid is a shadow of what it so clearly is here, is ridiculous and insulting. Have you found sufficient initiative to examine the bonnet closely enough to ascertain the size and nature of the dent on it?'

'It has been removed and sent for repair and painting. Yet Emilio described the dent as so minor as to be almost undetectable and the work seemed unnecessary.'

'You have spoken to the *planchista*?'

'I thought it more important to report to you first.'

'Have you inspected the bollard into which Tyler claims to have driven the car?'

'Not yet, because—'

'There is no need to repeat your inane excuse. You will inspect it immediately and report to me by early afternoon.' The line went dead.

The order might be impossible to fulfil in the given time. There was a good chance Nieto had sent the bonnet to a local known to be very skilled. But if he hadn't, he was going to have to be persuaded to say where it had gone. If neither bribery nor threats succeeded, there was the chance Emilio could find out the answer. Yet that might mean buying him more drinks at a front café and the cost involved still shocked. The English were to blame for his woes, Alvarez thought gloomily. Why could they not live and holiday anywhere but in his area?

As Alvarez came down the stairs, Dolores, who had been watching the television, looked up. 'What's wrong?'

'Nothing,' he answered.

'Then why are you down from your siesta so early?'

He stepped on to the floor. 'The superior chief demanded I make enquiries and report back to him by early afternoon.'

She looked at her watch. 'Then you have already disappointed him.'

'My enquiries will prove to be long and difficult. Is there any coca to have with coffee?'

'Would it not be better to forgo eating and drinking so you can return to work now?'

'Better for whom?'

She sighed. 'As my mother used to say, a man cannot look beyond his stomach.'

'There is a joke about that . . .'

'I do not wish to hear it.' She stood, went through to the kitchen.

Stress, he reminded himself, could kill. He sat.

'It's in the kitchen,' she said, as she returned to her chair.

She should have brought it to him. Where would the nonsense fostered by the ridiculous concept of equality of the sexes end?

Twenty-two minutes later, he left the house and drove

around the village. By the *torrente* – now dry and with a bed of pebbles and occasional rocks but after a prolonged rain, dangerous – was a large wooden shed which had the sign '*Taller Monroig y Hijo*' above the open doors. A non-descript building which failed to suggest the high quality of the work that was carried out inside.

He entered; no one was visible. 'Benito!' he called out.

A man, lying on a trolley, propelled himself from under an Audi with a battered offside. He came to his feet, partially cleaned his hands on a rag, shook hands, asked how the family was. Eventually, Alvarez explained the reason for his visit.

'That's right. Emilio brought it along. I told him it wasn't worth the doing, but the señor who owned the car had said it had to be repaired. If a man wants to waste money, why stop him?'

'Have you still got the bonnet here?'

'Sent it off to the paint shop this morning with the other panels.'

'Will they have done the job by now?'

'Like as not.'

'Would you phone and find out and if they haven't, tell them not to start work until I've spoken to them?'

'Is there something wrong with you phoning them?'

People no longer enjoyed the pleasure to be gained from helping others. Alvarez switched on his mobile and spoke to the *jefe* at the paint shop. The bonnet had already had several coats of paint, especially brought out from Palma, but was to get two more. Had anyone ever been asked to do so much unnecessary work?

Alvarez terminated the call. 'You examined the panels and bonnet carefully?'

'Just got hold of a sledgehammer and straightened 'em,' Benito Monriog said sarcastically.

'Any signs of damage that was not caused by concrete?'

'No.'

Alvarez returned to his car, sat behind the wheel, did not immediately start the engine. Heat sapped all the energy out of a man.

He arrived at Es Teneres forty minutes later.

'What is it now?' Tyler demanded.

'Señor, I should like you to tell me the address of your friend who owns the house at the entrance to which is the concrete bollard you unfortunately ran into.'

'Are you suggesting I lied about that?'

'I doubt you did, since it will be so easy to check. I should be grateful if you will tell me the address.'

'Ca'n Mahon.'

'Which is where?'

'Parelona.'

'Thank you.'

Alvarez returned to his car, sat, stared through the windscreen. Parelona. A small bay within the large bay of Llueso. Crystal clear water, sandy beach, a view through the headlands; luxury hotel, set in sculptured gardens, built when access had to be by mule track or water because there was no road, no luxury homes so expensive that only millionaires or drug dealers could afford them; paradise when there were few trippers. But paradise was only reached through hell. The drive from Port Llueso was over mountains and on roads which were bordered by sheer rock faces, occasionally used to commit suicide. A normal man found the drive tricky. For Alvarez, an altophobe, the drive was a continuous disaster about to happen.

He reached the level beach road and continued along that to the summer café where he drank a nerve-restoring brandy, then another to help him forget he would have to repeat the nightmare drive back to Llueso.

Ca'n Mahon, a large house with arched patios on the eastern side of the small bay, was six metres above the sea to which access was by a flight of stone steps. The house lay below the level of the road. There was an open drainage ditch, a metre deep, alongside the road, and two concrete bollards marked the edges of the bridge over this. The right-hand one bore signs of contact and a careful examination showed smudges of grey paint.

The office was hot and the fan did little to cool it. He studied the calendar and to his surprised pleasure found it

was Friday. Pleasure and pain were seldom parted. The
calendar was turned to the wrong month and it was Thursday.
Two full working days before the weekend.

He phoned Palma, informed the secretary who he was,
waited.

'It is a seldom enjoyed pleasure to hear from you,' Salas
said.

Alvarez silently sighed. It was a bad sign when the superior chief resorted to juvenile sarcasm. 'I would have phoned
earlier but—'

'You had difficulty in finding someone who could answer
your questions; your car broke down and you could not
phone for help because your mobile needed charging; or
did you trip and fall, twist your ankle and have only just
been released from the medical centre?'

'I first spoke to the *planchista*, señor. The panels and
bonnet had been sent to the *pintura*. The *jefe* there expressed
his surprise at the number of coats of paint which had been
demanded, but with a car of such amazing quality—'

'Contain your desire to deliver another panegyric.'

'The depression on the bonnet was not readily visible. It
was roughly circular and that would, of course, respond to
contact with part of the victim's body, perhaps the head.
On its own, that evidence carries very little weight, but
together with all the other evidence—'

'You were asked to ascertain facts, not deliver conclusions which lie beyond your capabilities. Is that all you
have to say?'

'Yes, señor.'

'You will make a full written report and fax it to me, to
be on my desk immediately. Once I have ensured it is
comprehensible and have corrected your grammar and
spelling, it will be sent to England. One last thing. Do not
bother to try to tell me this evening that I have not received
your report because the fax machine has failed.'

Alvarez replaced the receiver. A long and arduous task
lay ahead, made all the more unwelcome because there
seemed to be no way of escaping it.

SIX

August was hot; as hot as any recorded. In Alvarez's office, the fan was turning at maximum speed, but he was sweating so hard that his shirt stuck to his back.

The phone rang. After a while, he answered it.

'Woken you up, have I?'

A comedian. 'Who's speaking?'

'When we were young, you threw stones at Fat Lucía to make her swear, which she did better than any man.'

'Jaume! The same old liar. I have never thrown stones at a lady.'

'Not a memory the noble inspector wishes to remember?'

'What do you want?'

'A friendly chat.'

'When you—'

'Woke you up?'

Alvarez laughed. 'You always were a bastard!'

Conversation became less confrontational. The health of each other's family was discussed, past youthful escapades were remembered. Jaume explained he had been living in Ibiza from the time he had married Cecilia until she went off with another man; he had recently returned to Mallorca and had started working for a firm which delivered parcels all over the island. Alvarez expressed his commiserations for Jaume's marital loss.

'No need to shed tears. Years looking at the same woman over breakfast dulls a man's imagination. Eloisa brightens it up . . . I was going to get in touch to suggest a drink together, but right now I'm ringing because I was delivering a parcel and when I braked to a stop in front of Es Teneres—'

'Where?'

'Old age making you deaf?'

'In Val de Teneres?'

'Yes. Anyway, out through the front door rushed a young woman in hysterics. Took time to calm her enough to understand she had gone into the library and found the owner on the floor, with blood on his shirt and shorts . . .'

'Señor Tyler?'

'Some name like that. I went in to make certain she wasn't hallucinating, then called emergency. The duty doctor from the health centre arrived, said the man was dead – which didn't need brains to decide – and that he had apparently been shot.'

'Shot?'

'Must you repeat everything I say?'

'Shot where?'

'In the stomach. Twice.'

Suicide? Conscience could overwhelm even the corrupt soul. 'Was there a gun on the floor?'

'No.'

'Under his body?'

'Why are you going on about a gun?'

'To confirm it was suicide.'

'When the doc reckoned the Englishman had been murdered?'

'Why the hell didn't you say so at the beginning?' Salas might have said that. ' Have you called the policia local to put a watch on the place?'

'No.'

'Who's in the house right now?'

'The cook's away, ill in bed with something or other, so it's just the maid. The gardener turned up and wanted to know what was going on. There's no more to tell, so I'll be on my way.'

'You'll wait until I arrive. And make certain no one goes near the library before a policia arrives to take over.'

'I've a job to finish.'

'Which you can when I'm satisfied you didn't do the shooting.'

Jaume expressed his feelings in basic Mallorquin.

Alvarez smiled as he replaced the receiver. Jaume would

assure himself that the possibility he might have shot the
dead man was a tasteless joke, made in retaliation for
suggesting Alvarez had thrown stones at an elderly woman
when young, but there would be a corner of his mind which
would worry he might be suspected . . .

He phoned Palma.

'Yes?' Salas demanded.

'Señor, I am ringing to report that Señor Tyler has been
found dead.'

'Who?'.

'You will remember we were asked by England to question a Señor Cyril Tyler—'

'Since there were two Tylers involved in that matter, a
responsible officer would have taken the trouble to make
certain it was clear as to which one he was referring.'

'Cyril Leo Tyler. He lives . . . *lived* in Es Teneres and was
suspected of having driven his car into two young people
in England. Tyler—'

'You intend to deliver a résumé of the case?'

'I thought—'

'Unlikely. Where did he die?'

'In his house, here, on the island.'

'Why does his death concern you?'

'The doctor – he is not certified for forensic work. At
least I presume he isn't.'

'Why?'

'He was the doctor on duty at the health centre. He went
no further than to say Tyler had been shot twice in the
stomach.'

'You have waited until now to inform me this is a case
of either murder or suicide?'

'I doubt it is suicide . . .'

'I prefer to wait for an opinion from someone on whom
reliance can be placed. You have called for a forensic
doctor?'

'Of course, señor.'

'Have you searched for a gun?'

'Not yet.'

'You fail to understand the necessity of doing so?'

'I am here, not there.'

'Where is "here" and where is "there"?'

'I am in my office at the post.'

'Why?'

'I have only just heard of Tyler's death.'

'And you see no reason for conducting an immediate investigation?'

'You have always said you require a report to be made at the first possible moment.'

'A report requires facts. You have offered none beyond the fact of a probable shooting. You will go to the home of the dead man and learn the forensic doctor's verdict. You will search the house and grounds, question the staff, neighbours and anyone else who might be able to help. Then, and only then, will you be capable of making a report of any value.'

Alvarez gloomily wondered how he could return home in time for his meal. One could only be gratified to learn Tyler was dead, but why couldn't he have chosen a more convenient time and method to die?

As Alvarez braked to a halt, Jaume hurried out of Es Teneres and across to the Ibiza. 'Have you walked here?'

'Does it look as if I did?'

'Then buy a car with an engine. Do you know how long I've been waiting when I've work to be finished before I can knock off?'

Alvarez climbed out of his car. 'If you don't have to continue through half the night, every night, you don't begin to understand what work is. Has the policia arrived?'

'A sight sooner than you.'

'Where is he?'

'Hanging around in the hall, trying to get me to bring something out from Palma for nowt.'

'Let's get inside out of the sun before you tell me what happened.'

'You think I'm going to stay now you're finally here?'

'Unless you don't care if I begin to wonder why you're in such a hurry to leave.'

'No one told you a joke gets stale quicker than yesterday's paper?'

They went into the house. The policia who had been pacing the hall came across and they briefly chatted before Alvarez stepped into the library, which was very cold, thanks to the air conditioning having been set to a low temperature and working for a long time.

For once, he was able to look at violent death without suffering the inescapable fact and accompanying fear that all life must end, including his own. Convinced Tyler had been the driver of the car which had killed the young couple in Kent, he studied the body with equanimity.

Tyler, dressed for heat and not the cold of the room, had probably been sitting on the far side of the elaborately inlaid kneehole desk. A chair was on its side on the floor – knocked there as he fell or struggled to drag himself up? His eyelids were slightly open, and he might have been beginning to smile. The manner of death was not always apparent in a face. The cotton shorts and the silk sleeveless shirt had been stained with blood.

Alvarez visually searched the room. No gun was visible. A laptop on the desk was at an angle which allowed him to note the screen was blank. Not switched on because there had not been time? Nothing apart from the chair appeared to be out of place; the books neatly filled the bookcase and provided a sign of genuine or implied learning.

He walked slowly, carefully around the room, checking spaces which had not been visible from the doorway. The papers on the desk were filled with handwritten figures and indicated innumerable calculations. Pursuing moves to ease the problems to which Tyler had referred in his interview?

A crumpled piece of paper under the central space of the kneehole desk caught his attention. He bent down, picked it up and smoothed it out. A receipt from a supermarket. Meaningless. He scrumpled it up again and was about to throw it into the waste-paper basket when it occurred to him that if he replaced it, it could provide evidence to convince Salas that his search had been a very thorough one.

Miro, one of the photographers employed by the police,

entered the library. They chatted for a while before Miro took photographs at Alvarez's orders. To Miro's annoyance, Alvarez asked for three photos, taken from different angles, of the receipt under the desk.

Miro had just finished his initial task when Dr Font, whom Alvarez had met several times, arrived.

'Inspector . . . ?'

'Alvarez, Doctor.' Font's sharp facial features suited him. Visit him because one felt unwell, but lacked definite symptoms, and one would be met with sharp irritation.

Font put his small, well-worn leather case down on the floor, crossed to the body and studied it. 'Well?'

'Cyril Leo Tyler. He drove over from England in the first week of July. The maid came in here, found him lying where he is, and became hysterical. The driver of the van that's outside reported the shooting.'

'You have already diagnosed he was shot?'

'Not me,' Alvarez said with some satisfaction. 'The doctor from the health centre. It was his opinion that Tyler had been shot twice.'

Font opened his case, brought out surgeon's gloves and carried out an external examination of the body. He twice measured its temperature, checked movement of arms and legs, spent minutes closely examining the two wounds.

He stood, peeled off the gloves. 'There are no injuries other than the two gunshot wounds. No doubt you are going to ask for a time of death. That rigor is not yet appearing in the face and the blood temperature suggest a time of about two to three hours ago. However, the temperature of this room will have, to a considerable extent, interrupted the normal processes of decay. How long has the air conditioning been on at the present setting?'

'I'm afraid I can't say.'

'It would have helped to know.'

Was he, Alvarez wondered, supposed to have done what he did not know he would be required to do?

'Any estimate of time of death in this case, even when the question regarding the air conditioning can be answered, has to be very unreliable.'

'Can you say from what distance the shots were fired?'

'There are no contact wounds and the entry holes are split by the tail-wagging of the bullet. The range, as one can verify from the room, was less than fifty metres. The degree of soiling from the bullets implies a distance of at least one metre. There are no exit wounds and the bullets remain in the body. Lividity shows the body was not moved at any length of time after death.'

'The two wounds seem to be rather far apart.'

'Well?'

'Wouldn't one expect the gunman to have fired the second shot as soon as possible after the first?'

'If one ignores other possibilities such as spacing making it more likely a vital organ was hit, or that nervousness hindered an immediate second shot.'

'You're saying the killer was nervous?'

'I am saying no such thing.'

'But it's likely?'

'You would prefer to draw your own conclusions?' Font closed the case with a snap. 'I expect to hear details of when the air conditioning was switched on as soon as possible.' He lifted up his case, left.

Alvarez picked up the chair behind the desk and sat. He phoned the undertaker. He felt cold for the first time in weeks, even months, and was about to get up and leave, when Jaume entered.

'Happy, are you? Doing what you like best, sitting on your ass and staring into space?'

'I am contemplating the various facts so far ascertained.'

'More like wondering what you're meant to do next. I have to finish my job, so I'm away.'

'Have you spoken to the maid?'

'Julia.'

'Is she still hysterical?'

'No more than any other woman. Wanted to chat to someone, so I listened for a while. From what she said, it was seeing the bloodied clothes which upset her, not him being dead. If you ask me, she won't be laying flowers on his grave.'

'I doubt anyone will.'

'He was a bastard?'

'As big a one as you'll ever meet . . . We'll move in to another room and be more comfortable.'

'Didn't you hear me say I'm away to finish work?'

'When you've told me what happened.'

'I have.'

'Over the phone and disjointedly.'

'You were wrong when you said the dead man was as big a bastard as I'd ever meet.'

Neither of them looked back at the corpse as they left.

Once seated in the sitting room, Alvarez said: 'Describe what happened when you arrived.'

'I blew my nose.'

'Makes a change. Did Julia come out of the house before you braked to a stop?'

'You want to know, did she walk, trot, run? What's it matter if she came out on her hands? You don't give a damn how long I'm kept here.'

'What makes you so keen to work?'

'You won't understand even when I speak slowly. It's a sense of duty.'

'More like a penalty from your pocket if a parcel isn't delivered inside the guaranteed times.'

'You mind is malevolent.'

'Conditioned by experience. Now, start describing.'

'I drove in and stopped . . .'

'Who else was around?'

'Only the gardener.'

'What was he doing?'

'Gardening. What the hell do you expect him to be doing?'

'Carry on.'

'Julia came out of the house, shouting and screaming. Took time to understand what it was all about, then I went into the library. Phoned one-one-two and you and that's it.'

'Where did you go when you were in the library?'

'Over to where he was lying.'

'Did you pass to the right or the left of the desk?'

'God knows.'

'Did you touch the body?'

'I reckoned from the look of him he had to be dead, but I still felt for a pulse.'

'Did you move the body?'

'No.'

'It's lying exactly as it was when you first saw it?'

'If no one's rolled it around.'

'Where was the chair?'

'On the floor.'

'You didn't knock it over by mistake?'

'Most of us aren't as bloody clumsy as you.'

'Did you search for a gun?'

'Wasn't doing your job for you.'

'Were there any empty cartridges on the floor?'

'No.'

'But you didn't specifically look for any?'

'How many more daft questions are you going to ask?'

'Who other than Julia was in the house?'

'No one. I told you, the cook was away, ill.'

'Away where?'

'How the hell do I know? At home, I suppose.'

'The staff don't live in?'

'You learn fast.'

Alvarez brought a pack of cigarettes out of his pocket. 'D'you smoke?'

'Offering something in your old age? I don't smoke and you'd be more of a man if you didn't.'

'I am not old. Where was the chair when you entered the library?'

'You've just asked.'

'I'm interested to find out if you give the same answer.'

Jaume stood. 'You think you're going to question everything I've already told you just to show what a great man you'd be if you weren't filled with wind?'

'I never threw a stone at Fat Lucía.'

'If I'd the time, I'd remind you of Magdalena.'

'Who?'

'You never knew a Magdalena, I suppose, and it wasn't you who explained to her how a ram tupped a ewe.'

As Alvarez watched Jaume leave, he tried and failed to remember a girl named Magdalena. Probably he should check for fingerprints. He should question Julia and oversee the removal of the body before he considered leaving. But even if Julia had calmed down, it would be kinder not to bother her until tomorrow. Help would be needed to check the possibility of prints. The undertakers were very efficient and he could tell the policia to receive them.

Authority lay in the art of delegating.

Jaime was at the dining table, an empty glass and a half-filled bottle of Bach in front of him.

Alvarez sat, brought a glass out of the sideboard, reached across the table for the wine.

'Go easy,' Jaime said.

'Why?'

'That's all there is. She hasn't bought any more.'

'Didn't she check how little was left before she went shopping?'

'Says the cost of living has gone up so much, we're going to have to drink a lot less.'

'She'll have to cut back on something else.'

'Would you like to explain on what?' Dolores demanded as she stepped through the bead curtain.

Were women born with the ability to hear what it was intended they should not, or did they cultivate it? 'Surely we can make some little economies?' Alvarez asked.

'Indeed. Which is why I have not bought more wine and coñac.'

'I was thinking more of—'

'My clothes? You would like me to continue wearing my old clothes until they are darned and stitched and I am mistaken for a beggar?'

'Of course not.'

'Then you are thinking of food? I should spend all morning, however much my back and legs ache, visiting every shop to find where I can buy the cheapest meat, fruit and vegetables? You will be content to eat no better than the *menu del dia* at the meanest restaurant? Or maybe you are satisfied that there would be no difference from the meals I have been serving you?'

'The Ritz in Madrid can't produce food as good as you do.'

'Because I have the vanity of a woman, I buy creams to tend my complexion, mistakenly believing the men of the house wish me to look fine. You would like me to forgo my one small luxury in order that you may walk amongst the clouds?'

'You don't understand—'

'I understand that men are by nature selfish and will sacrifice anyone but themselves.' She returned to the kitchen, head held high, shapely shoulders squared.

'You would upset her before she's finished the cooking, so maybe she doesn't take proper care, wouldn't you?' Jaime said bitterly.

SEVEN

'Señor,' Alvarez said over the phone, 'I am about to type out my report and fax it to you, but—'

'You have found a novel reason why this should be impossible?' Salas asked caustically.

'I thought I should first explain verbally what I have learned.'

There was silence.

'It seems you have learned very little,' Salas remarked.

'I was waiting for your comment, señor.'

'You have just received it.'

'I meant, whether you would like me to make an additional verbal report?'

'"Like" suggests choice.'

'Font – the forensic doctor – confirmed death was from two shots; neither was contact. He gave the estimated time of death, but added that this was even less reliable than usual because the air conditioning was on in the library and set very cold. If it had been working since Tyler died – which has to seem probable – the cold would have delayed the usual sequence of post-mortem effects.'

'Was it on when he died?'

'I haven't yet been able to find out.'

'It was optimistic of me to think you might have done.'

'This definitely was not suicide because—'

'In face of your certainty, I suggest one accepts it might well have been.'

'The shots were fired some distance from the body and there is no gun in the library.'

'The forensic doctor was of the firm conclusion that it was a case of murder?'

'Yes.'

'Then he agrees with you. Not a welcome situation for a man of learning. You have questioned the staff, relations, friends to discern the motive?'

'Not yet.'

'Perhaps you do not think that necessary?'

'I haven't had the time—'

'Time travels at different speeds for different persons. For you, it seems always to be slow.'

'There has been so much to do, señor.'

'And so little done. Whom do you intend to question this evening?'

Alvarez looked at his watch. It was after seven, time for a pre-supper drink, but the superior chief was oblivious to such facts. 'It seems to me it will be best to start talking to the staff.'

'Then do so. You are viewing them as suspects?'

'Not at the moment.'

'Why not?'

'I have not yet had a chance to speak to them. Yet from what I've learned, I very much doubt Julia was the gunman . . . is that right?'

'Only if one is sufficiently incompetent to start a case with preconceived judgements.'

'I wasn't really meaning the question in that sense. What I was thinking was, if she had shot Tyler, she would not have been a gunman.'

'Why not?'

'Surely she'd be a gun-woman?'

'There are times, Alvarez, when I am convinced that you were accepted into the Cuerpo due to a malign mistake. You will question everyone at the first opportunity.' Salas rang off.

The first reasonable opportunity was the next morning. He would return home.

There was no answer to his knocking on the front door of Es Teneres. It was unlocked, so he opened it and stepped inside, called out. After a while, Julia came through a doorway into the hall.

'Hullo. You'll remember me. Enrique Alvarez. We met when I came here last.'

She looked blankly at him.

'I'm Dolores's cousin.'

She said a meaningless, 'Yes.'

Her appearance marked her as still being upset. She had not combed her hair, probably had not washed her face, the apron she wore had been secured unevenly, her manner was disorientated. 'I hope you're up to telling me one or two things I need to know,' he said quietly.

She looked briefly at him, then back at the floor.

'Suppose we find somewhere to sit and have a chat?'

She might not have heard him.

He walked over to the door of the sitting room, said in an authoritative voice: 'Come in here.'

She followed him inside, sat when he suggested she did so.

'What I'd like is for you to tell me in as much detail as you can remember, what happened yesterday morning.'

'No,' she said shrilly.

'I need your help to find out who shot the señor.'

'I don't know anything.'

'But you knew the señor.'

She said nothing.

'Not a very nice man from all accounts. And remember what he was like the first time I came here? Far too important to bother to be pleasant.'

'It's not right to talk when he's dead.'

'Death doesn't turn an unpleasant man into a pleasant one. He spoke to both of us as if we were ignorant peasants. It can't have been much fun working here.'

'It wasn't.'

He had finally gained her interest.

'I told Rosalía I couldn't stand any more. She said I was stupid. He wasn't here much of the time and all we had to do was keep the place clean; I wouldn't find another job as easy . . . Not that she wasn't always saying what she thought of bringing all those women to the house.'

'Is Rosalía the cook?'

'Been ill for three days now. I had to cook for the señor and he kept saying it was awful . . . It was his last meal.' Her voice rose.

'Did he bring a lot of women here?'

'Yes.'

'And that upset Rosalía? Is she very strait-laced?'

'Always thinking nasty and you know why? Jealous, that's what. No man's ever wanted to dent a mattress with her. Goes on about Pablo and me all the time. Not that there's any reason to do so.'

'Of course not. Were the women English?'

'Most of 'em. Except for the French woman who dresses like . . . like she was on the catwalk. If I ever wore some of the dresses I've seen her in, Rosalía would shout "puta" at me for what I was showing.'

'It's fashionable to be generous.'

'Her man can't think much of her since he don't care what she shows.'

'She's married?'

'And the husband's rich if all the jewellery on her is real. You'd have thought he'd take more care to know what she's up to.'

'Who is she?'

'Her name's Sophie.'

'Sophie who?'

'Never heard her called anything else. Rosalía knows, but all she ever says to me is, "What a slut!"'

'You've not met the husband?'

'Rosalía says he was with her the first time she came to a party, but I didn't see him. And seeing the time she spent here, maybe he's not around any more.'

'Were any of the other girlfriends married?'

'One or two were, but I can't rightly say more. Every time one of the marrieds turned up, Rosalía went on and on about him being so wicked, he had one foot in hell already.'

The fate of anyone who enjoyed life? 'Do you know the names of any of the marrieds?'

'One of them was like Raquel.'

'Rachel?'

'Could be.'

'What was her surname?'

'Wouldn't know. None of them had anything to do with the likes of us.'

Clearly there were several husbands who had good reason to dislike Tyler intently. 'Tell me about yesterday.'

Her nervousness returned.

'When did you start work?'

'I suppose it was maybe seven thirty . . . I slept a bit late.'

'That can happen, especially in the heat. Since Rosalía was ill at home, did you prepare the señor's breakfast?'

'When he phoned down to say he wanted it, I made the toast and coffee.'

'Where did he eat?'

'Had breakfast in bed and it didn't matter if he had one of his women with him.' She briefly sniggered. 'Wasn't half a laugh, seeing them trying to hide their faces.'

'What did you do during the morning?'

'Started cleaning the downstairs rooms. Didn't have to worry about lunch since he said he was going out.'

'Did anything unusual happen during the morning?'

'No.'

He was about to ask her another question, when she said: 'Hang on. I don't seem to be able to remember anything now . . . Four people came early and said they wanted to speak to the señor.'

'Male or female?'

'Two of each.'

'Did you know them?'

'No.'

'What did you do?'

'Asked them their names and one of them told me, used the internal telephone to tell the señor.'

'What was the name?'

'Can't remember.'

'It'll come back to you soon. When it does, tell me. Did the señor come down and speak to them?'

'Said I was to tell them to go away or he'd have them thrown off his land.'

'An odd way to behave.'

'He was often like that.'

'Perhaps he was afraid the two men were husbands with reason to see him.'

'Can't say.'

'How did they react when you told them he wouldn't see them?'

'They talked excitedly and argued, then left.'

'Talked in what language?'

'English.'

'Could you understand what they were saying?'

'I did English at school, but they talked too fast.'

'They argued, so perhaps they were very upset by his refusal?'

'One of 'em was. Acted like she was going to come in and see him whatever I said, but the man with her persuaded her to leave.'

'They drove away?'

'Yes.'

'Can you say what make of car they were in and what its registration number was?'

She shook her head.

Was this an event of some consequence, or of none? The most likely explanation had to be that they were two married couples who had known Tyler in England and were hoping to be entertained by him. He had refused to meet them, because he disliked them or was annoyed by the obvious attempt to milk his hospitality.

'Have you ever seen a gun in the house?'

She shook her head, fiddled with the edge of her apron.

'Did you hear the shots?'

She shook her head again; her lips were tight as she tried to control her emotions.

Es Teneres was built with thick walls of stone, so sound would not travel. If she had been in a room well away from the library, she would not be expected to hear them.

'After the two couples left, you did not hear or see anyone enter the house?'

'No.'

If the intruder had entered quietly, there was no reason to doubt she would not have heard him.

'There's nothing more to ask you, Julia. It's been very brave of you to tell me what you have . . . By the way, is Rosalía still ill?'

'She's back at work and looks like nothing's the matter, but if you listen to her, she ought to be in hospital.'

She hurried out of the room. He, more slowly, made his way to the kitchen. He introduced himself to Rosalía, asked her how she was, heard a list of symptoms from which she was suffering. Like so many of her generation, she would be flattered to be called merely 'plump'. A youth of hardship and later an ever-increasing abundance of food had tested her self-control and found it wanting. Her face was lined. By the age of eight, she would have worked in the fields, digging, weeding, irrigating, helping her family earn a poor living from the smallholding of land.

She stood by the double-oven electric stove, on the ceramic hobs of which were a casserole, a frying pan and a saucepan of boiling water. Since cooks sought and responded to praise, he said: 'Something smells delicious.'

There was no reaction.

'Is it a special meal?'

'With him dead?' she asked sarcastically. 'I suppose you think we don't have to eat?'

'Then you are all going to eat ambrosia.'

'Never heard of it. Potaje de garbanzos y espinacas, that's what it is.'

He was surprised, since the smell had suggested something far grander. Chickpeas remained chickpeas however they were cooked. Even Dolores had to work hard to make them palatable. 'I'm having a chat with everyone to learn what happened.'

'Then find someone else to talk to while I do the cooking.' She dropped several leaves of spinach into the boiling water.

'I've already had a word with Julia.'

'That girl has only one thought in her head.'

'She mentioned the señor quite often entertained ladies.'

'She knows too much about entertaining.'

'She thought some of the ladies were married.'

'There were three who even lacked the shame to remove their rings.'

'There was one lady who came here quite often.'

'Many came far too often, to their eternal damnation.' She dropped cut onions and carrots, three spoonfuls of chick-peas and stock into a blender.

'She was French.'

'*Mujer de las persianas verde!*' She started the blender and for a while, speech was impossible.

If he was to gain her cooperation, it was clear he should express his abhorrence of all that had happened. When the noise ceased, he said: 'I can't begin to understand how any woman could act as I'm told she did.'

Rosalía poured tomato sauce and the contents of the blender into the casserole, crossed to the double-door refrigerator and brought out four eggs, which she put in the boiling water with the spinach.

'The señor can have had no thought for her husband.'

'What adulterer has? He believed he had the right to take whatever he wanted.'

'The myth of money.'

'You think she is a myth?'

'Seems too obvious to be that.'

'She dresses to expose.'

To what extent? Not a question to ask now. 'Was it his money that attracted the women?'

'Without it, he would have been lucky if a *zorra* would have looked at him.'

'So I suppose he might have been killed by a husband seeking revenge.'

'If any of them was man enough.'

'Did you hear the shots?'

'When I was lying in my bed at home, wracked with pain?'

He apologized for his stupid mistake. He was surprised when, after adjusting the temperature under the casserole, she said: 'Would you like some coffee?'

'That would be very kind of you.' He had won her favour by his attitude towards extramarital relations.

Moments later, she poured out two mugs of coffee, crossed to a cupboard and brought out a silver sugar bowl, to the refrigerator for a plastic bottle of milk. 'You look like a man who enjoys his food.'

He accepted that as a compliment. 'I certainly do.'

'Then try one of the señor's biscuits.'

She put a round tin on the table, removed the lid.

The biscuit, coated on one side with dark chocolate, was delicious. 'Where did you get these?'

'The señor bought them.'

'From a local supermarket or one in Palma?'

'You think he did his own shopping? You do not know that a man like him would never carry a shopping bag because it makes him as ordinary as everyone else? It was always me being told what to get and me being cursed when it wasn't exactly what he wanted.'

'Then where did he get them?'

'From England, by post.'

'Must make 'em expensive.'

'Of what account is that to a man with a fortune?'

'And you reckon it was the money that attracted the women?'

'Do *putas* not work for money?'

'I wouldn't know.'

'Have another biscuit and save your tongue from nonsense.'

He was surprised she had spoken without aggression. Perhaps she held to the old standards. An unmarried woman had to be chaste. A young man needed to learn. He said, as he slid another biscuit out of the tin: 'Julia told me the French woman's Christian name was Sophie, but—'

He was interrupted as Rosalía again expressed herself on the morals of that woman.

Eventually, he was able to ask: 'Do you know her surname?'

'Douste.'

'She lives locally?'

'You think I wish to know?'

'You might have heard her say something to suggest whether she does.'

'She does not bother to speak to the likes of us. I remember
. . .' She became silent.

'What?'

'As if I was to blame when the electricity failed,' she
said bitterly. 'When the oven was not working for a while,
my cooking was ruined. I am an Andaluce and can cook
the best Pato a la Sevillana in the land. But that . . . that
putonga laughed as she wondered if the duck had died
of old age. I had to serve as well as cook because Julia
was ill, or so she said. Of course, Pablo would also have
been away from work. Her lust makes a good woman
cringe.'

'The young of today have no standards.'

'They have the standards of the debauched. When they
are called, they will be rejected.'

Along with very many others. 'The Frenchwoman had
the insolence to criticize your cooking when she should
have commiserated with you? Unforgivable! Did she speak
in French or Spanish?'

'French when she didn't want me to understand.'

'Yet you understood her?'

'Did I need to, when she had had only two mouthfuls
before she put down her knife and fork and said something
which made the señor furious and ask me if I was stupid
enough to think they liked raw duck?'

'She should have eaten, whatever she thought of the meal,
in order not to insult you.'

'What would a woman like her know about good
manners?'

'I wonder what kind of a man her husband is?'

'He is not a man to let her come here. He has no
cojones.'

'I don't suppose you've met him?'

'Where do you think the *puta* and the señor met? Here,
at one of the parties to show what a great man he was.'

'Did you speak to the husband?'

'A foreigner would not wish to speak to me when he
knows I am a cook.'

'In England, there are cooks who are said to be celebrities.'

'Anything can happen in a country where young girls behave as they do when they come out here for a holiday.'

'What kind of a man would you judge him to be?'

'That is not obvious? I have not already said? He is weak and stupid to allow his wife to come here on her own.'

'Perhaps he suspected what was going on, but didn't do anything about it so that he could share in what she gained.'

'Only a black mind could have such thoughts.'

'I fear my job exposes me to many evils.'

'Men expose themselves.'

'I don't think . . .' He stopped; best not to point out the ambiguity. 'Is he older than his wife?'

'Much older. She sold her body for what money he had. She sold herself to the señor for more.'

'I wonder if the señor has left her anything in his will?'

'Such a thing is possible?'

'I've known it happen.'

'Then you meet much stupidity as well as debauchery.'

'Has he heirs?'

'I only know that he was once married.'

'His ex-wife has been here?'

'Men do not bother with women from their past.'

'He could have children?'

'He would never have acknowledged them.'

'You are very critical,' he said, before he realized the injudiciousness of his words.

'No more critical than he deserves.'

'I'll need to find his will to discover if there are any heirs. I suppose there's a safe in the house?'

'I have been told it is in the library.'

He had not seen evidence of one. 'Do you know whereabouts?'

'I do not concern myself with such matters.'

'Perhaps you'll help me try to find it now?'

'Leave my cooking so that it is spoiled, as my Pato a la Sevillana was ruined?'

He was surprised she should compare duck to chickpeas. 'That was forgetful of me.'

'Men find it easy to forget.'

'Maybe Julia could help me.'

'That would be unusual.'

'Where is she now?'

'She should be cleaning the breakfast room.'

'Where's that?'

'Next to the library.'

Julia was vacuuming the traditionally patterned Sadhestan carpet which brought colour to the small room.

She switched off the Dyson.

'I've just had a word with Rosalía,' he said.

'Small wonder you don't look happy. I suppose she moaned about what she thinks me and Pablo get up to?'

'She didn't mention either of you. I need to ask if you know where the safe is?'

'Why me?' She spoke defensively.

'Because you might be able to tell me, since you clean everywhere.'

'But why d'you think I know where it is?'

'Do you?'

'What if I do?'

He said quietly: 'What's bothering you?'

She didn't answer.

'You're worried I might think you'd been up to no good? You're not that kind of a person. In any case, I'll bet you don't even know the combination or where the keys are?'

'Of course I don't.'

'Then there's as much chance of your opening a safe as of Rosalía finding a man.'

She smiled uneasily.

'So tell me, where is it?'

She explained at length that she had not been intentionally snooping, She had been dusting the framed prints on the wall of the corridor, as she always did. The door into the library had been open – it needed to be pulled hard to catch the tongue of the lock or it responded to any sudden draught and slowly opened – and she had seen the señor moving a book and pressing something behind it. To her astonishment, a section of bookcase had swung back.

'I cleaned in there ever since I started working, but I never thought there was something behind all the books.'

'It's a way of making a fairly secure hiding place. You can show me which section of shelves opens?'

'Me go into the library? I can't.'

'Forget what you saw.'

'All that blood on him. The terrible pain . . .'

'He died so quickly, he cannot have felt any.' Which was stupid talk. No one could know how death was met. Since life was painful, dying might be agonizingly more so, even when the transition, to an observer, seemed to be instantaneous.

'I won't go in.'

'All you need to do is show me where to look.'

'No!'

He spoke softly, explained that the señor's murder must be solved and that she might be helping him identify the murderer.

Not aware of what she was doing, she took his hand as they left the breakfast room and walked along to the library; her hand gripped his more tightly as they stepped through the doorway.

'Which part of the bookcase moved?'

She pointed.

'And roughly which book did he take out?'

'On the second shelf . . . I must go. Rosalía said I had to clean the dining room because it was so dusty. It isn't, but I must do that or she'll be awful.'

'You deserve a large coñac, so pour yourself one.'

'I don't drink.'

Small wonder she was so nervous. As she hurried away, he crossed the library to that part of the bookcase she had indicated. The movable section had been made with considerable skill and it would have been easy to miss its presence. He lifted out books along the second shelf and behind the third leather-bound volume of Churchill's *The Second World War* there was an electrical switch. He pressed it and the section of shelving swung open almost silently.

The safe was not a combination one; on the door was a

brass plaque on which was the name of a well-known maker. Top quality, burglar resistant and not just fire resistant. The simplest way of opening it to see what it held would be to ask Salas to authorize the employment of a professional locksmith. But Salas would demand to know if he had searched for the keys, hidden by Tyler. In a house of this size with rock walls, possible hiding places were endless and it might take hours to find the keys or claim the authority to say that forcible entry was necessary.

It would soon be supper time.

EIGHT

'I have to go to Inca tomorrow morning,' Dolores said, as she returned to sit at the dining-room table, having carried dirty plates and cutlery out to the kitchen. She reached across to the bowl of fruit and brought out an orange. 'Someone can drive me there.'

'Why?' Jaime asked.

She began to peel the orange, using a small steel knife. 'Because the times of the busses do not suit me. Because – not that you would understand this – a good husband always does what his wife wishes.'

'Half the time, she wishes so much he'd need four arms and four legs to cope.'

'You are attempting to be humorous?'

'No.'

'Then you succeed by failing.'

'How's that?'

She carefully separated segments of orange.

'Half the time I don't know what you're talking about,' Jaime complained.

She ate a piece of orange.

'Why d'you want to go to Inca?'

'Do I have to account for my every action?'

'I've a right to know.'

'You have no such right.' She ate more orange. 'But I will tell you. I am going to Inca to look at refrigerators.'

'Why?'

'Because I wish to buy one.'

'Why?'

'You have a very limited vocabulary.'

'But we have one in the kitchen.'

'Which is not working as it should.'

'We can live with it until it packs up.'

'At which point, it will no longer be keeping everything

inside fresh. That does not concern you until you collapse
from food poisoning and are rushed to hospital and have
to admit your error?'

'I can't see why—'

'Rosa has told me there is a large store in Inca which
has a sale of refrigerators, and one can buy a new model
for considerably less than here.'

'That'll all be nonsense. She gets everything wrong.'

'Indeed. When she first knew you, she remarked what
an interesting man you were.'

'We can't afford a new one.'

'And why do you say that? You were late back. Because
you spent even more time than usual at a bar?'

'I didn't go near one.'

'That is possible when there are two in every street? That
is likely when you again tripped over the front doormat as
you tried to enter?'

'The mat is in a silly place.'

'Then I will move it so that when your legs no longer
listen to your brain, you will come to no harm.'

'God Almighty—'

'How dare you blaspheme in this house!' she said fiercely.

Alvarez reflected that Jaime had still not understood that
the way to content a wife was to agree with everything she
said, accept with humility, guilt for every peccadillo she
wrongly alleged.

Jaime reached for the bottle of San Asensio.

'You suffer the desire to drink even more?' she said.
'Then I suggest you do not move from here until the clouds
have left your mind and you will be able to see the
doormat.'

He hesitated, finally poured himself a small measure of
wine. Alvarez took the bottle from him and refilled his own
glass.

She held a segment of orange in front of her mouth.
'Enrique, you are silent.'

'I have had an emotionally exhausting morning.'

'The bad luck to be told she wasn't that kind of a girl?'
Jaime suggested.

'You consider it bad luck to meet a virtuous woman?' Dolores asked sharply.

'It's just ... I mean ... I was being humorous.'

'Only in your own opinion.' She turned to Alvarez. 'What has been so exhausting?'

'Persuading a woman to do what she was afraid of doing because—'

'I wish to hear no more.'

'I had to ask her to go with me into the library in which she had found a dead man the previous morning. Naturally, she was unwilling.'

'They always are to begin with,' Jaime observed.

'As my mother so often had reason to say' – Dolores's words were coated in ice – 'a man's mind can only concentrate on one subject.'

Jaime was at fault with his blundering responses, Alvarez thought. If they needed a new refrigerator, one must be bought. Long gone was the time when refrigerators were rare and kept in the *entradas* as social statements. He chose a peach, cut it in half, eased out the stone ... Why should the word 'refrigerator' exercise his mind? The need to remember to pay his share of the purchase price? ... Air conditioning! He had to find out how long it had been turned on in the library. For once there was reason to be grateful for Jaime's manner, since it had saved him from forgetting to do what Salas was bound to ask if he had done.

Saturday morning. The beginning of the weekend. Only he was faced with having to work.

He drove to Es Teneres and as he turned in to the drive, saw a man working. He stopped, left the car, crossed the lawn – how much water was wasted to keep it green? – came to a stop by a flowerbed filled with colour – how much water was wasted on that? – spoke to the man who knelt, weeding by hand. 'Are you Higuero?'

Higuero slowly stood. He was short and stocky; although not young, his black hair was thick; his features suggested a bovine nature, but his blue eyes were sharp and contradicted that; his skin was tanned by sun, wind and rain; his clothes would not have been welcomed anywhere.

'Are you asking?'

'Didn't it sound like that?'

'Then you can say who your are.'

Higuero's manner would have annoyed most in authority, but Alvarez accepted it with amused tolerance. Contempt for authority had sustained the Mallorquins through invasions, poverty, oppression, civil war and the suppression of their language. Higuero's speech marked him as being from Mestara. The distance between there and Pollensa had once been a considerable mule ride, not lightly taken, and this had resulted in different accents and slightly different vocabularies. The journey could now be made in twenty minutes by car, yet the difference remained, largely because of a sense of local pride. 'Inspector Alvarez, Cuerpo.'

'Wouldn't have guessed it.'

Higuero's sharp eyes confirmed this was an insult. The butting goat must be expected to butt. 'Do you work here?'

'I look to be on holiday?'

'What do you do?'

'You're as thick as you are short-sighted?'

'I might have thought you were a gardener except the garden doesn't look as if one's employed.'

Higuero hawked and spat. 'There's some can't tell they're standing in pig shit.'

'And there are some who can't believe they aren't.'

'I suppose you're going to tell me I shot the señor?'

'Did you?'

'Never had the chance.'

'Tell me about him.'

Higuero spoke at some length, echoing much of what Alvarez had already learned. Tyler had lacked any manners as they were understood by a Mallorquin. He had never said good morning, shaken hands, had a pleasant chat. He had demanded rather than asked; believed that when he paid a man's wages, the man should treat him with deference; had thought himself at least the equal to God.

'I've been told he liked the women.'

'And they liked his money.'

'Seems more than one of them was married.'

'Probable.'

'There'll be husbands with reason to hate him.'

'Not if they're English.'

'Why d'you say that?'

'Horses and dogs for them, not women. That's why they all look constipated.'

'Have you seen a husband lurking around the place, wanting to have words with the señor?'

'How would I know what he was about?'

'Then you have seen someone?'

'No.'

'Have you noticed a Frenchwoman who's said to be something special and has come here quite often?'

'The one with real nice tits?'

'Can't be certain about that.'

'Dresses like she costs a thousand euros and shows you a little of what you'll be buying. Look at her and you aren't thinking of anything else.'

'Sounds like her. Have you seen her husband?'

'The first time she was with a man. Older than her and looked exhausted just by thinking about it. She wouldn't have been with the likes of him if he wasn't paying all her bills. She needs a real man.'

'Have you applied?'

'On my wages? She'd just laugh.'

'Then your poverty saves you from committing adultery.'

'Who bloody well wants to be saved? Have you finished asking stupid questions?'

'I've one or two more.'

'Then they can wait until after.'

'After what?'

'*Merienda*.'

'At a local bar?'

'Rosalía makes coffee and something to eat.'

'And to drink?'

'What do you do with your coffee? Wash your feet in it?'

'I was thinking of something stronger.'

'From the looks of you, that and women is all you do think about.'

'Maybe I could join in.'

'Why?'

'Am I not subject to the same hunger, the same thirst, satisfied by the same measures as you?'

'If you ask me, you've been on the bottle all morning. I wouldn't give someone from the Cuerpo a crust of dry bread, but Rosalía can be soft.'

'Thank heaven for soft women.'

The coffee was strong, the apricot *coca*, made that morning by Rosalía, as tasty as any Alvarez had previously enjoyed. They discussed the señor's death and what it might mean to them and it was late morning before they decided it was time to move.

'I need another word,' Alvarez said to Julia as they stood.

'What about?'

'Nothing to cause you any worry . . . Mateo,' he called out as Higuero stepped into the outside doorway and sharp sunshine.

'What?'

'I'll talk to you again.'

'Not if I can help it,' was the muttered response.

At Alvarez's suggestion, Julia and he went into the breakfast room. She sat, fingers locked together on her lap.

'I only need to know one thing,' Alvarez said quietly, his tone friendly. 'When you went into the library and tragically found the señor dead, was the air conditioning on?'

She looked through the window, her fingers now tightly clenched, her expression strained.

'Was it working?'

She finally nodded.

'At what time of the morning did you switch it on?'

'I didn't.'

'Have you any idea who did?'

'Must have been the señor. We weren't allowed to touch any of the units. He said only he was to do that.'

'Do you know why?'

'Some time ago he was out to lunch and not supposed to be coming back until the evening, so I turned the air conditioning off in some of the rooms to save electricity. He returned unexpectedly soon after lunch with a woman and created hell because the rooms weren't very cool.'

In the circumstances, that surprised him. 'So as far as you can tell, no one will know when the unit in the library was switched on on Thursday?'

'No.'

'Then that's all I need to know. Thanks again for your help.'

She left.

He would report to Salas that despite a long and very thorough investigation, there was no way of being certain how long the air conditioning had been switched on in the library, but there was strong reason to accept it must have been from before Tyler was shot. So the time of death as given by Dr Font had to be as unreliable as he had warned.

He walked a couple of times up and down the library for the exercise, recognized he had to make some sort of a search for the keys before he reported to Salas that the safe could not be opened until a locksmith was called. He opened the desk drawers, checked through their contents, replaced these. He removed books near the one hiding the control of the moving section of shelving to determine if any of them had been hollowed out to provide a reasonably good hiding place; none had. To show keenness, he got down on hands and knees to look under the central gap in the desk and to his surprise saw two keys fixed to the underneath of the bridging top. Why hadn't he noticed them when he'd previously looked under the desk and found the supermarket receipt? Could the keys have been visible in the photos that were taken of the receipt? If so, Salas might . . . He pushed the possibility to the back of his mind.

In the safe were several coloured files, portfolio valuations, statements from banks in England, Liechtenstein, and Llueso, accountants' reports, a will, just over a thousand euros in notes, *escrituras* of land and house.

The will was very straightforward. All that Tyler owned

at his death was to be donated to a named charity. An attempt to buy his way into heaven? So either no one had murdered him in order to benefit financially, or someone had been mistaken about the contents of the will. To decipher the full meaning of the pages of bank balances and investment portfolios was beyond Alvarez's ability and he doubted anything would be gained from doing so. Nowhere had he uncovered what he had hoped to find – something to verify the accusation that Tyler had been driving the car which had killed the two young lovers.

He replaced the contents of the safe, locked that, returned the keys to their hiding place; if any of the staff had sought for and failed to find them in the past, they were unlikely to try again; in any case, Llusians, unlike Mestarians, were totally honest.

He returned to the kitchen where Rosalía was preparing lunch. He debated the amount of garlic there should be in a *suquet de pescado con allioli* and for the sake of peace agreed two whole cloves should be sufficient. He said goodbye, left, was approaching his car when there was a shout. Higuero crossed in front of several mimosa trees, came up to the car. 'You said you wanted to talk, but I ain't seen anything of you. I ain't waiting around any longer.'

'You have business elsewhere?'

'Nothing to do with you what I have.'

'Let's go back into the house where it's cool.'

Muttering his annoyance, Higuero followed Alvarez inside and into the breakfast room.

'Take a seat,' Alvarez said.

'Don't need you to tell me what to do.' Higuero sat.

'I asked you if you'd seen any husbands out for revenge lurking around the place and you said you hadn't.'

'You want to call me a liar?'

'Men from Mestara are noted for their honesty.'

'And when they go to Llueso, they stitch their pockets up. Why tell me what I told you?'

'Just setting the scene.'

'What scene?'

'Thursday. The señor was shot and I have to find out

who shot him. Considering his mode of life and love, an angry husband seems a likely suspect, so I'm asking if you've thought things over and remembered someone who's been around and looked suspicious on any previous day.'

'I told you, there was the car.'

'You haven't told me about a car.'

'I bloody well did!'

'Then tell me again.'

'I was coming back to work and it come out of the drive like it was racing.'

'What time was this?'

'After lunch.'

'So it was some time after four?'

'Two.'

'You'd eaten by two and were returning to work? Get any funnier and I'll have you inside.'

'The señor said I had to work in the afternoon from two to six.'

'Why?'

'Them was the hours he was used to in England.'

'You didn't tell him this was Mallorca?'

'You don't spit on your own plate.'

'He paid so generously you did as he said, instead of telling him you would work as a Mallorquin did?'

'Who are you to talk when you're with the police and so always have to do what you're told?'

'What was the time this car drove out on to the road?'

'Didn't I say I was getting back to work at two?'

'So what do we suggest? Half past two?'

'When the señor was likely watching to see I was dead on time?'

'He kept a sharp watch on you?'

'Suspicious bastard.'

'No doubt because he was used to the ways of workers in England. So you could only be a little late. Twenty minutes?'

'It weren't nearly that much.'

'Give me a figure I can believe.'

'Maybe ten past.'

'What made you notice the car?'

'Because he came out so fast, like I said. If I hadn't swerved violently and fallen off my moped, he'd have had me.'

'It was a man driving?'

'Just said.'

'Did you recognize him?'

'When I only seen the back of his head?'

'Was anyone else in the car?'

'Didn't see no one.'

'Did you take the number?'

'Tried to, so as I could denounce the sod.'

'But failed?'

'You think you can see much when you've just missed being slaughtered by a car?'

'You were suffering from shattered nerves?'

'Weren't like that,' Higuero replied angrily, not prepared to admit that a man from Mestara could be so craven. 'It was well away when I got myself back on me feet. All I could read was the numbers, not the letters. Eight-five-three-three.'

'You're certain?'

'I've said what I remember.'

'Did the letters come before the numbers?'

'Yes.'

'Can you suggest what any of the letters might have been, even if you're not certain what they were?'

'No.'

'What kind of car was it?'

'Estate.'

'Make?'

'Astra, most likely.'

'Colour?'

'Black.'

'Any signs of damage, any stickers in the back window?'

'Nothing.'

'If you think you see it again, take the number and let me know.'

'You finished?'

'For the moment.'

Higuero stood. 'Any more questions and you can answer them yourself.' He left.

Alvarez considered what he had heard. The car had left the grounds of Es Teneres soon after two o'clock. It had been driven recklessly. Because the driver had just shot Tyler and was panicking? That would put the time a little outside the estimated time of death, yet Font had admitted this was even less reliable than usual because of the coldness of the room and now it was known the room must have been cold at least from the time of death. If luck was on his side, all that remained to be done was to identify the car and its owner. How false were his dismal forebodings with which he had started the investigation.

NINE

'Identify a car from what you've just told me?' said the man in Vehicles over the phone, speaking as if asked to perform a couple of miracles before lunch.

'Is it going to be difficult?' Alvarez managed to sound concerned.

'Won't take more than the rest of the week to find out it's impossible.'

'Aren't the computers working properly?'

'You think all we have to do is tap a couple of keys and out come all the answers?'

'I don't know very much about them.'

'Nothing, from the sound of it.'

'I'll have to report it's too difficult to follow up?'

'I'll see what can be done. But don't expect any answers in a hurry.'

Alvarez replaced the receiver, settled back in the chair. He felt sorry for the cuckolded husband who had shot Tyler. If there were honest justice, he would be held to have been justified, but laws were promulgated by men and therefore could never be just. He looked at his watch and regretfully decided it was still a little early to leave the office and return home for a drink and lunch. *Merienda* at Es Teneres had not included a coñac. Presumably, Rosalía disliked alcohol as well as men.

The phone rang.

'The superior chief,' Salas's secretary said, in her plum-laden voice, 'will speak to you.'

As he waited, receiver to ear, Alvarez wondered if she had ever been courted? If so, probably by a masochist.

'Are you there?' Salas demanded.

'Yes, señor.'

'Why have you not reported?'

'I am waiting to hear from Vehicles before I do so.'

'Why?'

'I can't get the information from any other source.'

'What is the information you require?'

'The name of the owner of the car.'

'What car, why is this important, and to what case does it refer?'

'The murder of Señor Tyler, señor. I have questioned the staff. Julia told me that no one was allowed to alter the air conditioning in any of the rooms—'

'Do you ever answer a question?'

'When I know the answer.'

'Which is seldom. I asked what car are you referring to.'

'The one which made Higuero fall off his mobylette. He says it was travelling so very quickly – as if it was racing, was his description – but I think one needs to remember that when one suffers a near miss that might have proved fatal, one is liable to exaggerate.'

'Where was he at the time?'

'Returning to Es Teneres after lunch. It was unusually early because Tyler demanded he worked to English times. Somewhat ridiculous, since this is not England—'

'I do not require you to remark on the obvious or to confuse by delivering an incorrect commentary on national habits. Why is the car of consequence?'

'Higuero was turning in to the drive when it came out at such speed and so carelessly that the driver was surely under drink or very confusing emotion. The time is important since the staff was not permitted to alter the air-conditioning settings . . . But I have mentioned that.'

'There are occasions when you speak in so confused a manner, I am at a loss to know if you have told me anything. One moment you were waiting to hear from Vehicles before you made your report, the next, a man was nearly run down and that is important, but your only explanation of why this should be is that the air conditioning couldn't be altered. You will start again, after you have arranged the facts in as logical a sequence as you are capable of doing. You will refrain from any observations which are immaterial. You will not offer any conclusions you have reached since these can only cause still further confusion.'

Alvarez carefully made a restructured report.

'It is unfortunate that one has to wait to learn about the driver of the car,' Salas said.

'It seems it's not as easy as one thinks to get a computer to work—'

'I was referring to the fact that I have only just heard about the car which drove out of Es Teneres's forecourt at a time which must cast suspicion on the driver.'

'Higuero didn't mention the car until this morning.'

'Because you had not questioned him about it.'

'How could I, until I knew about it?'

'My friend, the noted psychologist, may well express a wish to examine you. Not only would I be interested in his findings, he may use the details of your extraordinarily confused mind to propose a new syndrome which would bear his name. The would be an honour. Moreover, he would be able to enjoy the pleasure of appreciating that in a hundred years, his name will not be forgotten.'

'But what about my name?'

'Hopefully, that will soon be forgotten.'

'Isn't it likely to be quoted, so that people might well think I was mentally unstable?'

'The possibility is there, together with the reality. You will inform me the moment you hear from Vehicles.'

Alvarez replaced the receiver, leaned over and opened the bottom right-hand drawer of his desk, brought out a bottle of Fundador and a glass.

Vehicles phoned at a quarter past five. The speaker first expressed his opinion of inspectors who demanded miracles.

'I also have to work very hard,' Alvarez said.

'That's meant to be a laugh? I've a mate who says you haven't done any work since you joined the Cuerpo . . . There are a considerable number of black Astras with those last four figures so you're going to have to iden-tify the one which interests you.' That was spoken with satisfaction.

These days, it seemed everyone tried to shift their work on to other shoulders. 'If you could sort out the addresses into areas . . .'

'I could, but I'm not going to.'

'Superior Chief Salas has always said that for overall efficiency, all departments should work together—'

'Salas talks crap. I'm faxing the list through in five minutes.'

The list was not as long as Alvarez had feared, but was not nearly as short as he had hoped. It took him until seven to sort the owners into geographical areas. Gloom returned. It could not be assumed that the car belonged to anyone in his area, so he might have to extend the search. Unless he informed other inspectors that on the orders of Salas, they were to carry out inquiries in their areas.

On his way home, he stopped at the godown in Carrer Labarcena, well known for the quality of the fruit and vegetables it sold and, more importantly, its wide range of wines. He bought a couple of bottles of Isola, returned to his car and was about to drive away when he remembered Jaime and he had emptied the bottle of brandy after their previous meal. He returned to the store for a bottle of Soberano.

Alvarez studied the list of six local addresses. Two in the port; one a car hire firm; one midway between there and the village. One in the village, one in the mountains close to Laraix. Dolores had an acquaintance in Laraix whom he would be expected to visit, not because of friendship, but because she was a recent widow, owned an old house which had been renovated, and her husband was reputed to have left her a great deal of money having been the kind of entrepreneur whom Mallorquins respected – so tight-fisted, it was said his nails had grown into the palms of his hands. Susana believed alcohol to be the bait of the devil. He would not mention a trip to Laraix to Dolores. Of the two addresses in the port, one was near Los Dos Pescadors, an old-style bar and restaurant set back from the front, which welcomed locals by charging them less than the tourists.

*   *   *

He walked into the offices of Torrandell Rent-A-Car. It was a modern building and the three staff, one man and two young women, were equally modern and so seemingly uninterested in customers.

He banged the glass-topped counter on which were brochures detailing the first-class service the company offered. After he had studied Alvarez and with no difficulty identified him as Mallorquin, the tall, thin man with blond hair in a ponytail said in Spanish: 'Break that and you'll pay for it.' He switched to English. 'You half-witted goat.'

'A half-witted goat has some manners, unlike you,' Alvarez replied in English.

They stopped smiling as they recognized authority, even if not in uniform and uncertain what was the authority.

He switched to Mallorquin. 'Who's in charge?'

One of the young women indicated the man.

'I want some information.'

'It's all set out in our brochure—'

'Who rented this car?' He put a sheet of paper down on the counter.

'I'm not certain—'

'Then find someone who is.'

'Who . . . who are you?'

'Cuerpo General de Policia.'

'I didn't realize . . . You want to know who rented the car with the number you have there?'

Power might tend to corrupt, but there were times when corruption could be welcomed if it was to one's benefit. 'I've other work to do, so I'll return later for the name and address.'

'Hang on . . . I mean, could you wait a moment?'

'Why?'

'I've just read what you've written. You've only given us the numbers, not the letters.'

'Which is because I do not know what those are. But if you have a black Astra, or any other estate whose registration number ends in those figures, I want to know.'

Back in his car, he debated whether to drive to Los Dos

Pescadors or to walk since it was only two roads down. In the present heat, caution was necessary. He drove.

The bar had not been modernized, enlarged or altered to attract tourists; indeed, tourists were hardly welcomed since they tended to disturb the locals, although if they entered in search of local colour, they were served at front bar prices. Pensioned fishing gear hung on the walls, as did many old photographs of fishing boats and the men who had worked them. Three men had been circled in red. They had died at sea.

Thirty minutes later, he returned to the rental company, where his reception was markedly different and he was welcomed with smiles.

'I'm afraid we don't have a black estate, Inspector,' the blond man said, 'but we do have a dark green Astra which has the four figures you gave us in its registration.'

Alvarez scratched his chin, which reminded him he had not shaved that morning. 'Perhaps we were given the wrong ones.'

'Not necessarily.'

'Why's that?'

'A dark green can appear black when the sun's shining directly on it and at an angle.'

'Of course.' If he had ever known that, he had forgotten.

'I've had the name and address written out for you.'

The redhead – he regretted he had never had the chance of learning whether the reputation of redheads was justi-fied – handed him a sheet of paper. 'I've printed out the date when Señor Drew first hired the car, which he still has, Inspector.'

He thanked her, left, returned to his car for which he should have bought a parking ticket – since it was summer – but had not. No notification of a fine was pinned between windscreen and wiper blade.

Once seated behind the wheel, he reread the name and address. Timothy Drew, Aparthotel Vora La Mer, Port Llueso. Car first rented several days before.

To save making a U-turn in the face of considerable traffic, he went down to the small roundabout on the front, then back up the road to Llueso. He was almost up to the turning off to Cala Roig when he swore, using one of the more colourful Mallorquin phrases, braked to a sudden stop, causing a van behind him to pull out sharply. The driver shouted through his open window as he passed with horn blowing continuously. How, Alvarez wondered, could his mind not have immediately fastened on the significance of the name Drew?

TEN

'What's brought you here?' the cabo on the duty desk called out. 'Hasn't anyone told you it's a Sunday?'

Alvarez walked up the stairs a shade too quickly and had to pause for breath before entering his room. He sat. Above all, he must make it clear to Salas he had understood the significance of the name immediately. He had a little brandy to help his memory, phoned.

'Yes?' said a man.

'Is that the superior chief's office?'

'Did you dial his number?'

'Yes.'

'Then quite likely this is his office.'

'I was expecting to speak to the superior chief's secretary who is a woman—'

'That is a matter for discussion.'

'Presumably, she is away?'

'Yes.'

'And the superior chief is away as well?'

'No. You want to speak to him?'

'Not really.'

'Putting you through.'

'Yes?' said Salas, with his usual belligerence.

'Señor, I have—'

'Forgotten to name yourself yet again.'

'I thought you would have been told who was calling.'

'I was not.'

'I am Inspector Alvarez.'

'You imagine that is not obvious from your inability to follow orders?'

'Then . . .why ask who I am?'

'I have already made that clear. Why are you phoning?'

'I may have traced the car, which was hired.'

'What car?'

'Which drove out of Es Teneres on Thursday afternoon soon after two. That is within the window of time in which one can be fairly certain Tyler was shot. I have been in touch with Dr Font and given him the news about the air-conditioning unit—'

'How does that affect the car?'

'It doesn't. What I mean—'

'Memory tells me this conversation bears a strong resemblance to a previous one.'

'I don't quite follow that.'

'Do you follow anything? I then explained that when making a report, an officer must initially identify those about whom he is reporting and the reason for his doing so. Since my words have failed to trigger any response from you, it is probable I failed to put things sufficiently simply for you to understand.'

'I presumed—'

'It is presumptuous as well as irresponsible of you to presume.'

'Things can be difficult—'

'For you to do anything efficiently, impossible. Are you aware it is Sunday?'

'It has been mentioned, señor.'

'You see no reason for not wasting my time?'

Rest for whom?

'You will write your report instead of irritating me with mindless mutterings.'

'Señor, I think you should know right away there has to be doubt about the car even though its registration number does end in three-three-three.'

'As far as I am concerned, the car is in complete doubt since I have no idea as to what is your reference.'

'I have spoken to one of the firms in the port which hire cars and they have an Astra estate whose registration ends in three-three-three.'

'I am grateful to you for troubling to inform me of the fact.'

'There is a problem.'

'You surprise me.'

'The car in question is dark green, not black.'

'Then either the reported colour was wrong or one of the figures was.'

'Not necessarily.'

'You are introducing a new form of logic?'

'Did you know that in sharp sunlight, dark green can appear black if seen only briefly?'

'Of course.'

'Then why—'

'Well?'

'Nothing, señor.'

'I asked you only minutes ago to cease irritating me. Name the man who was driving the car.'

'Timothy Drew.'

There was a silence.

'You are unable to understand I might wish to know what his evidence is?'

'When I write my report—'

'I want to hear it now.'

'I haven't yet spoken to him.'

'Why not?'

'Because he is Timothy Drew.'

'You delight in non sequiturs?'

'I . . . I'm not certain.'

'Do you always hesitate to question someone because he is who he is?'

'But in this case I think he is.'

'Is what?'

'Timothy Drew.'

'Have you been drinking heavily?'

'It's odds on, señor, that he is the father.'

'Into what fields of incomprehensibility are you now about to stray?'

'Perhaps if I mention England?'

'Why not Easter Island?'

'England is the beginning.'

'You will reach the end as quickly as possible.'

'If you remember—'

'Your repeated inferences that I do not have an excellent memory have become insolent.'

'But I'm trying to be helpful.'

'You disguise that fact with skill.'

'One of the two people knocked down and killed by the car driven by Tyler in England was Irene Drew. It surely has to be more than a coincidence that there now is some reason to suspect a Timothy Drew of having shot Tyler.'

'To point out the obvious is only wasting still more time.'

'You didn't seem to follow what I was saying, señor.'

'You cannot understand why I might appear to see no connection between the names?'

'It seemed you didn't. Naturally, you would very soon have done so.'

'Your effrontery is obnoxious, your servile assurance, contemptible. Incredibly, I need yet again to explain, even if to do so will be as productive as filling with water a bucket which has a large hole in the bottom. I delayed commenting on the obvious in the hope that for once you would make an efficient report. I am an illogical optimist . . . I have as yet had no explanation as to why you have not questioned Drew.'

'I thought you should first be informed, since you would wish to consider our next move.'

'A man who drives wildly out of the grounds of a house in which a murder has just been committed does not immediately become a suspect? When it is learned he is the father of the girl who was mown down by a car driven by the murdered man, he becomes the prime suspect. Such a suspect is not to be questioned rigorously?'

'I am not so certain of all that.'

'Then I suggest you find a job in which your level of intelligence is acceptable.'

'How could Drew know who was the driver of the Bentley? The English police had sharp suspicions which, of course, is why they asked for our help, but they would never have named Tyler to Drew before Tyler was arrested.'

'Your mistake is to judge the English police as exhibiting

the same professionalism as the Cuerpo. You will question Drew.'

'Yes, señor.'

'Immediately.' Salas rang off.

On a Sunday, 'immediately' had to mean after a siesta and tea. He had hoped to have the pleasure of proving Salas had missed the significance of the name, but the superior chief had somehow managed to scorn the possibility and blame him for his inefficiency. He should have remembered that a mouse did not challenge a wolf.

Aparthotel Vora La Mer, on the corner of the road, was within two hundred metres of the beach. A pleasant, if artistically uninspired building, it was U-shaped with the two wings enclosing a large swimming pool. The noise from the swimmers reached into the office, to the right of the entrance doors.

'Drew?' said the manager, whose features bore the strain of coping with tourists.

'Timothy Drew.'

The manager ran a stubby forefinger down a column of names. 'Mr and Mrs Drew, suite G.'

'He has a wife here?'

'As you suggest, unnecessary. Many young ladies stay during the summer.'

'Where's suite G?'

'The last on the right as you go to the pool.'

He passed the restaurant and went into the open, walked down the right-hand side of the pool, in which were many children who, were one to judge from their cries, were killing or being killed. As he knocked on the door marked G, a heavy splash of water just missed him. He turned to see a young boy duck under the corner of the pool's edge. Children were a blessing, but not all were blessed.

The door was opened by a woman probably on the edge of middle age. Linen shirt and shorts made it obvious she maintained physical fitness. Her hair was brown, short, razor cut, her face round, her features pleasant but marked by a large mole on her left cheek. In the mysterious way in which

judgements were made, he became certain she was a woman
of warmth and compassion, possessed of an inner steel not
easily broken by the bitter episodes of life. 'Mrs Drew?'
he asked in English.

'That's me.'

'I am Inspector Alvarez of the Cuerpo General de Policia.
I should like to speak to your husband if that is convenient?' His words startled and shocked her.

'Why, what do you want . . .?' Her tone was shrill.

He didn't answer.

She began to overcome her panic. 'He's gone out. I'll
see if he's in the café.'

Sadly, he thought that if his investigation proceeded as
seemed likely, she was going to suffer further tragedy. No
judge could accept Drew had justification for Tyler's murder.
'I need to ask him a question or two,' he answered. It was
kindness, and perhaps a touch of cowardice, that had
prompted the meaningless answer.

'Please sit.' She left.

Through the window, which could be covered by a closed
Venetian blind, but had not been, he watched her walk along
the poolside. How much courage did it take to live after
the death of one's child? She knew the answer.

As he waited, he looked around himself. He was surprised
by the quality of the accommodation. The sitting room was
reasonably well furnished; through the open doorways he could
see, or infer, two bedrooms, a bathroom, and a small kitchen.
Unsurprisingly, aparthotels were becoming ever more popular
with tourists, ever more disliked by hoteliers. They offered a
family a financial saving compared to the cost of a hotel,
provided they did not eat out often. A wife might complain
about having to cook when on holiday, but that was her job.

Drew, wearing bathing trunks, closely followed by
Sandra, who was holding his hand, entered.

'My husband, Inspector,' she said.

Observing the strange custom of foreigners, Alvarez rose
to his feet.

'Sandra says you want to know something? Before we
find out what, may I offer you coffee or a drink?'

Reasonably handsome, brown curly hair not yet receding, high forehead, broad shoulders, no hint of a beer belly. 'Thank you, but no, senor.' In the past, he had had reason to wonder what the English used to make coffee.

'My wife was about to go out . . .' Drew began.

'No, I wasn't,' she said quickly.

'You're forgetting you had to buy something at the chemist.'

She looked at him, released her hand, unwillingly picked up a shopping bag and purse, left. Drew said he'd change quickly, went into a bedroom. He returned, sat, fidgeted.

'Would you mind if I have a drink?'

'Why should I, senor?'

'You've refused, so I'll be drinking on my own.'

Another illogical British taboo? 'If that distresses you, may I change my mind?'

'What would you like? If I haven't got it, I can nip into the bar and get it.'

'A coñac with just ice, please.'

'Nothing easier.' Drew stood, went through to the kitchen. When he returned, he handed across one of two filled glasses.

'You . . .' Drew stopped.

'Yes, señor?'

'You haven't said why you are here.'

'I apologize for being so remiss. As you may have heard, an Englishman, who lived not far from here, was shot dead on Thursday.'

'I didn't know.'

'Perhaps it was not in the local English paper.'

'I wasn't aware there was one.'

'And it may not have been mentioned on the television.'

'There's English telly in the lounge, but we haven't bothered to watch. We came here to relax.'

'You have been stressed?'

'Work becomes ever more difficult, thanks to a government whose aim is to eradicate profit. Why . . . why do you think I might have heard about the shooting?'

'I have come to ask if you knew the victim.'

'You haven't said who he was.'

'Cyril Leo Tyler.'

Drew shrugged his shoulders. 'The name doesn't ring any bells.'

'You have never met him?'

'No.'

'And you have not visited Es Teneres?'

'What's that?'

'The home of Cyril Tyler.'

'I would not have been to his home if I had never met him.'

'He might not have been at home which meant you did not meet him.'

'Why would I go to somewhere I'd never heard of to meet someone I didn't know?'

'It is a question which I hope you may be able to answer.'

'I don't understand what this is all about.'

'You cannot guess?'

'I'm English, he was English, so I must know him? Is that it? God knows how many English live here, but to the best of my knowledge, I haven't met a single one of them.'

'Have you rented a car whilst here?'

'Yes.'

'What make, type and colour is it?'

'A green estate. I think it's an Astra.'

'Were you out in it on Thursday?'

'We've been out in it every day. You said this man was killed on Thursday. Are you suggesting there's any significance in our having been in the car that day?'

'That is what I hope to find out.'

Drew drained his glass, stood. 'D'you want another?' His tone had become far less easy.

'Thank you, señor. As we say, August is a thirsty month.'

Drew left, soon returned, handed a glass to Alvarez, sat, drank.

'Where did you drive on Thursday?'

'As far as I can remember, into the mountains.'

'You took the Laraix road?'

'I can't say what road it was.'

'You did not visit the monastery?'

'We had a picnic in the mountains and then returned.'

'What is the car's registration number?'

'I don't know.'

'It ends in the figures 8533.'

'If you know, why do you ask?' Drew said with weak belligerence. 'Is the next question, "how many wheels does it have?"?'

'I can assume it has four.'

Drew looked out through the open doorway at the pool from which came the never-ending noise of fun. 'I'm sorry.' He spoke more calmly. 'As I mentioned, we're here to relax and all your questions are making me . . .' He stopped.

'I'm sorry you find them so disturbing.'

'It seems as if you think I might have had something to do with this man who's been shot.'

'You are quite certain you did not know Tyler, have never met him?'

'Couldn't be more sure.'

'And you have never been to his house?'

'No.'

'A dark green or black Astra estate was seen leaving Es Teneres shortly after two on the afternoon Tyler was shot. The four figures in the registration number were the same as those of your hire car.'

There was a long silence.

Drew finally said: 'What about the letters?'

'They were not noted.'

'Other cars will have the same numbers.'

A little exaggeration did not come amiss. 'I have checked every car on the island whose registration number contains those numbers and the only one is the green Astra estate you have hired.'

'You're trying to say it was my car?'

'It seems probable.'

'I'm saying, impossible.'

Drew had spoken with calm certainty. Strangely, now the accusation had been inferred, he had overcome his nervousness. 'Had you any reason for hating Tyler?'

'I'll answer that by repeating myself. I never met him, did not know of his existence until you told me about him.'

'It is possible to hate someone even if one has never met him.'

'In exceptional circumstances, perhaps.'

'These were exceptional circumstances.'

'Meaning?'

'Señor, it is with regret that I have to refer to the death of your daughter. She and a friend, Señor Newcome, were knocked down and killed by a drunken driver who never stopped. Tyler was the driver of that car.'

Drew stood, crossed to the outside window. When he turned back, his eyes were moist. 'I never knew who the bastard was. I asked the superintendent to tell me if he had any idea who he was. He said he could not give me such information. Until you named Tyler, I couldn't even guess who he was.'

A point Alvarez had raised with Salas. It had been dismissed by impugning the English police.

'And if you can still think I am somehow implicated in Tyler's death, Sandra and I had lunch with friends on Thursday and were with them from midday to late afternoon.'

'Why did you not tell me this earlier?'

'For a while, I didn't understand what this was all about; when I did, I decided not to mention them and have them upset by being questioned.'

'Surely it was obvious that if their evidence cleared you of any possible involvement, they would not have been worried?'

'As I am having to learn, being questioned is worrying, whatever the cause and result.'

'May I have their name and address?'

'You are determined to go ahead?'

'They will merely be asked to confirm what you have just told me.'

'My word isn't sufficient?'

'In a case such as this, I fear not.'

'Mr and Mrs Howes. They've rented a house called Guillet.'

'Whereabouts is that?'

'Camp de Mar.'

'A very pleasant area.'

'Will you do something for me, Inspector?'

'If I am able to.'

'Try not to upset them any more than is absolutely necessary.'

Sandra entered, a plastic shopping bag in one hand. 'Still here, Inspector!' She looked intently at her husband, her concern obvious.

'Only for long enough to say goodbye to you, señora,' Alvarez answered.

'I hope I didn't sound rude, but I thought . . . I see from the glasses, Tim remembered to offer you a drink.'

'Very kindly so, señora.' He thanked her and her husband, said goodbye, went out on to the pool patio. He looked back through the window of the room he had just left and although the harsh sunshine caused sharp reflections, was able to note the expression of frightened concern on her face as she spoke to Drew. Why? If they had been with friends at the other end of the island when Tyler was shot, they had no reason to be concerned. And surely they must have been with those friends because they could not be so naive as to imagine their claim would not be queried and the Howes would not be questioned?

He returned to his car. The evidence had been fitting together. Now, it had been ripped apart and scattered. He was going to have to start again, right from the beginning. A thought to drive a man to the nearest bar.

ELEVEN

'You have spoken to them and they confirm Drew's evidence?' Salas said.

'No, señor. Since Camp de Mar is not in my area, I assumed you would ask the local inspector to question them.'

'It is interesting how, purely by coincidence supposedly, your assumptions leave others to do the work. I will inform Inspector Malberti that because of the nature of this case, I wish you to carry out the interview.'

'He won't welcome me . . .'

'I should be surprised if he did, since he is a highly efficient officer. However, it seems to me that unfortunately the benefits of his conducting the questioning are fewer than the problems of your doing so. You will question Señor and Señora Howes immediately.'

'It is nearly six . . .'

'I am well aware of the time.'

'Camp de Mar is at the other end of the island.'

'It is to the east of Andraitx, not west, and Andraitx is not at the end of the island.'

'Roughly speaking—'

'I expect my officers to speak exactly.'

'The problem is the time it takes to get there. Well over an hour. Perhaps another hour to question the Howes and then I will have to return here. By then, it will be late at night.'

'It will be approximately nine o'clock. I am fortunate if I manage to leave here before nine every night.'

'That must upset your domestic life.'

'My domestic life has nothing to do with you.'

Rumour said Salas and his wife might share the same bed, but she had forgotten why.

'You will drive to Camp de Mar and question the couple now.'

'Very well, señor. But first I will phone them.'

'Why?'

'To make certain they will be there.'

'You have their number?'

'Señor Drew was able to give it to me.'

'Then you will pass it on to me and I will phone them and order them to remain at home until you arrive.'

'You don't expect that might—'

'I expect my orders to be carried out without question. You will wait until I ring you again.'

'Yes, señor.'

Alvarez slumped back in the chair. He stared across the office and through the unshuttered window at the sun-scorched wall of the building on the far side of the road. Camp de Mar was an expensive area. Wealthy foreign wives on holiday would not cook, preferring to eat in the most expensive restaurant within reach. He crossed middle and forefinger on each hand. The Howes would not be at home. They would have their meal overlooking a sea which was striped by golden moonlight, the breath of wind would bring them the scent of wild broom, heather, lavender, rosemary . . .

The phone rang.

'There was no answer,' Salas said. 'I imagine you have provided the wrong number.'

'It was Señor Drew who gave that to me so if . . .' He was talking to himself.

A man had to be lucky occasionally. He could return home, his conscience crystal clear. Dolores might be preparing something special and had he been unable to be at home to enjoy it, she would have been so annoyed she might not have paid as much attention to cooking the next meal as she should have done.

Camp de Mar was noted for the wealth of the expatriates who lived there and Alvarez had expected Guillet to be a large and luxurious house. It was not. It was a boxy bungalow built to a strict budget, with a plunge pool – swimming pool in estate agents' language – set in a plot of less than 500 square metres.

He knocked on the front door. It was opened by a young

woman with too much make-up, straggly hair, which was in fashion, scarlet finger nails, an apron over a short dress with generous décolletage. He introduced himself. 'And you are?'

'Eva.'

In his mind he recalled another, earlier Eva. Not a welcome memory. 'You work here?'

'And in five other chalets.'

'Are Señor and Señora Howes at home?'

'Yes. You want to see them?'

'After I've had a word with you.'

'Why?'

'You can tell me something.'

'Should've said there wasn't anything you didn't know,' she said archly.

The other Eva had also sung a siren's song. The song had ended abruptly. 'Were you working in this place Thursday morning?'

'Mondays and Thursdays it's another chalet.'

'But you might know if guests had been here to lunch on Thursday.'

'When I wasn't here?'

'There'd be a lot of extra tidying up, glasses, plates and cutlery to wash.'

'The machine does that.'

'Was it unusually full on Friday?'

'Almost empty.'

'Do the Howes usually empty the machine when it's finished its cycle?'

'Leave it all to me, like the rest of them. Expecting me to do everything while they just lie out in the sun.'

'Wouldn't you, if you were on holiday?'

'Do you or don't you want to see them? I must finish the job here and move on.'

'Have an English couple named Drew been here recently?'

'Could have done.'

'Hardly an answer.'

'Look, I rush around doing the work and there ain't the time for introductions.'

'The husband is in his late thirties or early forties, a metre

seventy to eighty tall, reasonably good-looking, wavy brown
hair, a beaky nose, and friendly.'

'No one's tried to pinch my bum recently.'

'You mistake the meaning of the word. His wife is a very
pleasant woman who suffers the misfortune of a large mole
on her cheek.'

'She's been here. Remember thinking, why doesn't she
have it removed?'

'Was she with her husband?'

'She was with a man.'

'When was this?'

She thought. 'Can't really say.'

'A long time ago?'

'Recent.'

'Tell me about them.'

'How d'you mean?'

'Did they greet the Howes like old friends?'

'I reckon they hadn't met before.'

'What makes you say that?'

'I suppose the way they just shook hands and the women
didn't kiss each other on the cheek . . . Don't you ever think
something and can't really say why?'

'Sometimes.'

'I can't stand around any longer. They're out on the patio.'

He passed through the very small hall into a reasonably
sized sitting room that was furnished cheaply, and out on
to the south-facing patio.

Howes, who had been lying on an air mattress, came to
his feet.

Alvarez hid his surprise. Howes was tall, lean, muscular.
Nothing surprising there since there were those who found
little pleasure in food and drink. It was his facial appearance that was remarkable. He had the sleek, smooth, suave
features of the male star in a romantic film in the days
before he was required to resemble a lumberjack. That he
was married could be a cause for surprise. 'I am Inspector
Alvarez of the Cuerpo General de Policia.'

'That sounds very impressive!' Howes smiled. Near
perfect white teeth. 'My wife, Kirsty.'

She had remained lying face down on a second air mattress; now, she turned her head and looked up. 'Hullo.'

A second reason for astonishment. Howes could be expected to marry superficial glamour. She was sufficiently unglamorous to be overlooked in a crowd of three. Her two-piece bathing costume was well filled.

'What have we done or not done to bring you here?' Howes asked.

'I only have to ask a few questions,' Alvarez replied.

'About what?'

Had Drew not rung Howes to say he would be asked to confirm the alibi? 'I believe you are friends of Señor and Señora Drew?'

'Indeed. But before we learn more, won't you sit?'

He moved across to one of the chairs, set in the shade of a sun umbrella fixed through the centre of a patio table.

Howes sat opposite him, asked: 'Why is our friendship of any importance?'

'I should like to ask when you last saw the señor and señora?'

'Yesterday. We drove over to have a meal with them.'

'And before then?'

'Has something happened to concern them and us?'

'I need to find out if it does.'

'Rather ambiguous.' He waited. When Alvarez showed no intention of speaking, he said: 'When did we see them before yesterday? Must have been on . . .' He turned to Kirsty. 'It was Thursday, wasn't it?'

'Yes,' she answered briefly.

'At what time did they arrive here?' Alvarez asked.

'That's a tough one since time doesn't exist on this island . . . It must have been around eleven. He had said they'd be earlier, but were late as usual.'

'How long were they here?'

'They returned some time after seven. I told them it was far too early and we expected them to stay for supper, but Tim talked about not wanting to drive in the dark – obvious nonsense since he could have stayed and still returned in daylight. There was something he probably wanted to watch

on television. He's a great telly fan, we're not – which is
as well because the reception here is not very good.'

'Thank you for your help,' Alvarez said. He stood.

'Nothing more?'

Alvarez smiled a negative.

'No hint about what the problem is?'

'I have just learned there is no problem.'

He said goodbye – she barely acknowledged this –
returned to his car. He had parked in the shade of a tree
with windows shut to avoid theft – by foreigners – but the
sun had moved on and was now shining through the rear
windows so that the interior was hot. He started the engine,
released the handbrake, drove off.

Drew's alibi had been confirmed and the car which had
driven away from Es Teneres had not been his. Higuero, who
stubbornly believed himself incapable of any mistake, had been
mistaken and the car probably had been black. Witness statements were so often flawed. People saw what they expected
to see, not what they did . There would have to be a second
attempt to identify the car which had driven away at speed.
The possible combinations of colour and numbers was all but
beyond calculation. He would leave Vehicles to sort them out.

A Porsche went past him at speed, had to brake sharply
for a corner. Yet another potential suicide. His thoughts
wandered. Howes had been helpful in an unctuous manner
which suited his appearance; his wife had been monosyllabic-
ally abrupt. Was that her nature?

'So Señor Drew could not have been at Es Teneres on
Thursday just after two o'clock,' Alvarez reported, having
returned to his office and recovered from the drive. 'A man
cannot be in two places at the same time.'

'You accept that?' Salas asked.

'Of course, señor.'

'I am grateful.'

'Higuero's evidence has to some extent to be wrong.
Unfortunately, there is great difficulty in judging what the
correct number might be . . .'

'Why?'

'The possible combinations are all but endless.'

'What other make of car can readily be mistaken for an Astra?'

'All cars look alike these days.'

'Only to someone who cannot be bothered to observe differences. Have you considered what figures become sufficiently indistinct at a distance that one might mistake one for another?'

'One wasn't in the number.'

'It is beyond your ability to understand that the first "one" I spoke was a pronoun, the second an unnamed but specific object?'

'Are you saying that at a distance a three can be mistaken for an eight?'

'How far from the car was Higuero when he misread the numbers?'

'I'm not sure.'

'You should be.'

'He was so shaken when he fell off his mobylette that whatever the distance, his judgement would be virtually valueless.'

'A man of very little self-control. We have three numbers to consider.'

'Four, señor.'

'Are the last two not the same? Can you suggest another number with which five can be confused?'

'I suppose with six, if written badly.'

'Were the numbers on the registration plate handwritten?'

'Of course not.'

'It amuses you to introduce irrelevances?'

'I just thought—'

'Of thoughts that haunt your thoughtless wilderness. You will assume that the make and colour of the car are wrong; that one or both of the threes were eights.'

'And perhaps the eight was a three?'

'Unlikely, since it is a case of visually subtracting body rather than adding. Nevertheless, you will do so.'

'It is going to be very difficult and take a very long time . . .'

'To be expected when the work is carried out by you. Is the man's eyesight adequate?'

'You mean, Higuero's?'

'You expect me to be referring to the driver?'

'I wanted to be certain, since you didn't refer to him by name.'

'Continuity of speech means nothing to you? On what grounds do you accept without question what Howes told you?'

'There was no reason to think he might have been lying.'

'You ignore the fact he is a friend of Drew?'

'I doubt someone would lie in a case as serious as this merely because of friendship. Although it is possible they aren't the close friends they seem to be.'

'What is your authority for saying that?'

'The maid, Eva, was present when the Drews arrived where the Howes are staying. She believes they hardly knew each other.'

'A couple were likely to drive the length of the island to meet someone they did not know?'

'Señor, you told me Camp de Mar was not at the other end of the island.'

'Your impertinence knows no limits. What this woman thought can be of no consequence.'

'But there are one or two people on the island who possess the ability to judge the truth in another's mind.'

'Peasant nonsense.'

'Not so, señor. Eva might be descended from Fernando. He lived in the mountains with his family and owned so little that when he travelled to the nearest village on his decrepit mule, the beggar in the village would jeer at him. He tried to farm, but the mountains are not friendly to farming and they were often hungry unless they managed to kill a feral goat, a rabbit or netted some birds. Yet even so, they often visited Damían, the anchorite, who lived in a cave at the foot of Puig Brot, and gave him food because he had even less than they.'

'What the devil is the point of all this?'

'I am about to explain, señor. Damían, just before he died,

said he wished to thank them for their kindness, but all he could offer was the gift of being able to read another's mind. He warned Fernando that such a gift was both good and bad. Fernando thought of the benefit he would have when trading the little produce he had to sell – he might be able to afford a bar of chocolate for his wife – and accepted the offer.

'Later, he felt unwell and his wife persuaded him to ride their sad old mule over the long and difficult journey to Laraix where he could consult a doctor, despite the fortune that would cost. The doctor told him there was nothing much wrong with him and he would be fine if he took some pills which he could buy at a *farmacia*. He read the doctor's mind and learned he might have cancer. When he returned to the cave in the mountains, he did not return to work, but lay down to die.'

'I do not expect my inspectors to pay heed to such nonsense.'

'It is fact.'

'You would like to explain how the power of extra-sensory insight was transferred? Was it with the wave of a wand or the flourish of a broom?'

'Fernando's wife left the mountains when he died and came to live in a tumbledown *caseta* just outside Llueso. Word soon spread she could read a person's mind and those who did not wish this were quick to see the *caseta* was renovated and she had wine and food.

'Tia María was never wrong. She said little Catalina was contemplating suicide because Tomeo had left her for another woman. Catalina's mother claimed that was nonsense since no woman could consider a man worth as much as a cut finger. Catalina threw herself down a neighbour's well and drowned, which was very inconvenient because the well had to be pumped out and it was summer when every litre of water is precious.'

'Have you finished?'

'I am trying to explain why one should be ready to accept Eva could be right.'

'Is Eva the daughter of this woman who can read another's mind?'

'Who would marry a woman who knew all one's thoughts? Tia María never remarried.'

'That is no hindrance to birth on this island. Alvarez, were you dropped on your head soon after you were born?'

'I have never been told I was.'

'It was probably hidden from you. You will ignore Eva's absurd claims.'

'But—'

'That is an order. You will concentrate on work, not ridiculous myth, and determine what car drove out of Es Teneres very soon after Tyler's murder.'

'Yes, señor.'

Alvarez replaced the receiver. Life was unbalanced. A man could do his best and yet be blamed for not doing better; he could point out a possibility and have it rejected with scorn. He looked at his watch. Time to return home. What would Dolores be cooking? Costelletes de porc amb salsa de magranes?

TWELVE

For the first time in days, there were clouds, bringing some slight relief from the heat; tourists complained, animals ventured out from under the shade of trees, hedges and walls.

In his office, Alvarez sat back in his chair, his feet up on the desk. He was depressed. If he continued to make so little progress in the case, Salas would accuse him of incompetence and demand he worked twenty-five hours a day; Dolores was in one of her womanly moods, possibly because Jaime was continually, if inadvertently, annoying her; Juan and Isabel were spending the holidays arguing with each other; and the government had announced an increase of the tax on alcohol.

Through the open window came the call of a travelling knife grinder. How long since he had last heard the sound of a conch shell being blown? When had anyone last threshed or winnowed; ploughed with a mule; driven a donkey cart along the roads; intensively cultivated a quarter of a hectare to keep a family fed? Small general stores, where one went for a chat as much as to buy, had largely been driven out of existence by the supermarkets. Brandy, gin and rum could no longer be sold from the barrel. It was not good to age. Old men – not that he was even middle-aged – did not forget; they remembered and memories were painful.

The phone rang. A *policia* in the port reported a tourist had had his pocket picked and accused a Romanian without papers. The Romanian swore by many gods that he had not stolen as much as a cent. There was nothing in his possession which could be determined to belong to the tourist. The inspector had better turn out to deal with the problem. Alvarez said he was engaged in a major investigation so had not the time to deal with a minor one and as the victim

was only a tourist, the *policia* would have to sort things
out.

He lit a cigarette. Salas had been scornfully contemptuous of anyone's having the ability to read another's mind.
Perhaps time had generously embellished the story, yet it
was undeniable that at times one could instinctively gain
an impression concerning the attitude of another and this
was as often true as false.

What if he accepted Drew and Howes had never met
before? Why would Drew have driven from Llueso to Camp
de Mar? It didn't make sense. Yet there had been the meeting
so it had to make sense. Again, accept Drew had shot Tyler.
Then one had to believe Howes' evidence – and his wife's
– regarding the luncheon party on the day of the shooting
was a lie. But why lie to support a stranger? Because they
had reason to shield Drew? They themselves had suffered
at the hands of Tyler? It had been their son who had been
killed by the drunken Tyler?

He had logically deduced the truth from what had seemed
to be irreconcilable facts.

He leaned over and opened the bottom right-hand drawer
of the desk. There were moments in life when a drink was
earned. He had just emptied the glass when it occurred to
him that the man who had been killed with Irene Drew had
been Blaise Newcome, not Blaise Howes.

There was only one way of meeting bitter frustration. He
had a second drink.

'You look like she changed her mind at the last
moment,' Jaime said, as Alvarez sat at the dining-room table.

Alvarez reached across for the bottle of 104, brought a
glass out of the sideboard, poured a drink. 'If only.'

'What?'

'It was that simple.'

'You've been caught?'

'I was so certain.'

'Never safe to be that. I can remember—'

'Remember what?' Dolores called out from the kitchen.
She stepped through the bead curtain. Her midnight hair

was in slight disarray, her face was sweaty, her apron was stained, but the scornful dignity of her expression was that of an extravagantly clad Andaluce rider at the great fair. 'Well?'

'I've forgotten,' Jaime muttered.

'Because a man only remembers what he wishes to.' She turned to Alvarez. 'You are in trouble?'

'Not just yet.' Jaime sniggered.

'You seek humour in the dustbin,' she snapped.

'To prevent further misunderstanding,' Alvarez said, 'I do not have a newly pregnant girlfriend.'

'But not for want of trying,' Jaime suggested.

'In this house you will speak as a man of decency, not as the man you are,' Dolores said fiercely.

She turned to Alvarez. 'What is the trouble?'

'I thought I could make a fool of the superior chief.'

'He needs no help to be that.'

'I imagined I was going to have the delight of explaining that there are times when I can be smarter than him.'

'If he were not from Madrid, he would not need to be told that.'

'I was so certain I had worked out the truth, but I had forgotten. I often forget. Perhaps he is right and I am not up to my job.'

'What foolishness are you speaking now?'

'I forgot the son has the same name as the father.'

'If he's lucky,' Jaime said.

'In your father's case, *he* was the unlucky one since you disgrace it,' she snapped. 'Enrique, of course he bears the same name, even if his father dies and his mother remarries.'

Alvarez stared at the small framed photograph of Dolores's mother wearing what had been the traditional dress of working women – *palmito* tied under the chin with coloured ribbon, black skirt reaching down to the ground.

'What is it now?' she asked, her concern increased by Alvarez's manner.

'I'd like to kiss you.'

'Can't keep him quiet,' Jaime said lightly. His mood

abruptly changed. He was going to have to buy a new
refrigerator.

Salas rang at a quarter to one, as Alvarez was about to leave
the office, convinced the other would not get in touch with
him that close to lunchtime. Were he a superior chief,
Alvarez would guard his digestion by always enjoying a
long luncheon break.

'I should like to know, Alvarez, why you have yet again
ignored the rules governing the conduct of officers?'

'I didn't know I had, señor.'

'Because you have never bothered to consult the rules?'

'What particular one am I supposed to have breached?'

'Which you *have* breached. No contact is to be made
with a foreign police force without the express permission
of the commanding officer.'

'You are talking about . . .' He did not name his call to
England since Salas could be accusing him of some other
breach of conduct which he might be able to explain.

'You made a request to the British police without reference to me. You were unaware that any such request must
be made through a senior officer?'

'No, señor, but—'

'You are about to try to excuse the inexcusable?'

'I thought the matter was so simple, my question could
be answered without the usual fuss.'

'Standing orders are not "fuss". They are the rules
governing the proper running of the Cuerpo.'

'I was trying to save you trouble, señor.'

'Your resignation would do that far more effectively. A
man in London has just replied by phone to your illegal
request for information, and due to your disregard of orders,
I initially had no idea as to what he was talking about. It
is extremely regrettable that he may have thought me far
from clear-headed.'

'Most unlikely, señor.'

'I did not ask for an opinion.'

'What did the Englishman tell you?'

'I will come to that in a minute.'

In five minutes, Alvarez thought. And in six minutes, I will expose the falsity of your criticism and the incompetence of your judgements.

'You doubted Señor Howes was providing a legitimate alibi for Señor Drew because you absurdly claimed the maid had read their minds and discovered they were not friends. It is an indication of the primitive intellect that it believes the impossible. So you failed to consider the circumstances and ask yourself, "What if by some coincidence, not mono-telepathy, they really had not known each other? Then what could their meeting signify?"'

'Señor, as a matter of fact—'

'Had you the ability to look beyond known facts and attempt a reasoned assumption, you might then have asked yourself, "Why should they meet, what could have caused them to wish to do so?" And that could have led you to consider the possibility that the meeting was in order they might claim friendship. Why should they wish that? The answer is clear – to me, at least. Because they had some common interest. Yet if they had never met before, what could that be? The necessity to provide a false alibi following the murder of Tyler, who had killed their respective son and daughter.

'The falsity of this conclusion should be obvious, but I will explain it. The female victim was Irene Drew; the male victim was Blaise Newcome.'

'Señor, I phoned England—'

'Without reference to me, in breach of the rules. Had Mrs Howes married a second time; had Blaise Newcome's parents died when he was young and he had been adopted by the Howes? England has provided the answer. Blaise's father died and his mother married Señor Newcome.

'Señor Drew has attempted to arrange a false alibi and that is a strong indication of his guilt in the murder of Tyler. Have you been able to follow all I have said?'

'Señor, I phoned England because—'

'You phoned without my permission.'

Alvarez accepted defeat.

'Do you understand what to do now?' Salas asked.

'Yes, señor.'

'You will question Drew far more vigorously than before, you will re-examine all evidence in order to note the important facts which, in your slapdash style, you have until now ignored.'

'But there is actually no hard and fast evidence against him. So shouldn't I also try to identify and question husbands of the wives Tyler has entertained?'

'It is astonishing you find it necessary to ask. You should already have identified and questioned such men. You will not use the word "entertain" in connection with the moral crime of adultery.'

'No, señor. What worries me is that I cannot see Señor Drew shooting Tyler.'

'Had you done so, this investigation would have been unnecessary.'

'Judging his character, it is very difficult to visualize his committing murder.'

'You judge character as easily as some woman of primitive background is supposed to read the mind?'

'I see him as a man who accepts life is cruel and so can reconcile himself to tragedy.'

'You have a son or daughter?'

'I don't think . . .'

'What were you going to say?'

'I don't think parenthood is important.'

'If one's son or daughter is killed by a drunken driver who then tries to escape justice, you imagine a father can accept the tragedy without emotion, without hatred for the driver?'

'There's a difference between hating someone and killing him.'

'As great a difference as between an efficient officer and an inefficient one. Have you found the gun used to kill Tyler?'

'No, señor.'

'Have you even conducted a second search for it? Have you questioned the staff to determine whether they ever saw Tyler with a gun? Have you questioned anyone who might have sold it to Drew?'

'I have made a second and very thorough search, señor, spoken to the staff, and passed the word around to know who's dealing in guns. The search revealed nothing, the staff have never seen a gun. I have not yet had any information from informers.' As he spoke, it occurred to him he had not questioned Higuero about guns. 'If he had possessed a gun—'

'Who had?'

'Señor Drew. That would show premeditation. This might seem to be corroborated by the fact that the meeting between Drew and Howes took place before the murder of Tyler – Drew was establishing an alibi should one be needed. In this case, obviously the murder was carefully planned. But I don't think it went anything like that. Señor Drew is not capable of planning and then executing a murder. He might, as might anyone, shoot if provoked beyond self-control, but that is all.'

'Your authority?'

'As I said earlier, his character—'

'And as I have had reason to say endless times, an officer relies on facts, not an unqualified judgement of character. Is that clear?'

'Yes, señor.'

Salas did not say goodbye. Alvarez replaced the receiver. After lunch, and a siesta, he would have a word with Higuero so that it became fact no one had seen a gun.

He left and was halfway down the stairs when he heard the phone in his room begin to ring. He continued on down.

He returned to his office and sat. The black clouds of the morning had been dispersed by a couple of brandies before a dish of *patatas con sepias y almejas*, a glass or two of wine and a prolonged siesta.

The phone rang and the plum-voiced secretary said the superior chief wished to speak to him.

'Where have you been?' was Salas's greeting.

'In what way, señor?'

'What kind of an answer is that? I wished to speak to you shortly after doing so this morning, yet there was no answer.'

'I suddenly received information which suggested a man could tell me about the illegal sale of a small handgun, so I left the office to make contact with him.'

'The result?'

'The report proved to be nonsense.'

'I phoned at four this afternoon and again there was no answer.'

'When I discovered the informer knew nothing of import-ance, I returned to Es Teneres and yet again searched the grounds. Unfortunately, once more without success. I hadn't realized how long that would take and did not return home for lunch until late in the afternoon. I ate as quickly as I could and returned here.'

'I am surprised to learn you are so devoted to your work.'

'I have always held that if a job is worth doing, it is worth doing well.'

'That has not previously been obvious. Do you know why I am ringing now?'

'Not really.'

'You are unaware you have ignored a most important point in this case?'

'Which one?'

'You have ignored so many you cannot decide the one to which I am referring? How did Drew know Tyler was on the island and where was his house?'

'You may remember I did pose that question—'

'Had you raised it, you would by now be able to answer it. Can you?'

'Not precisely.'

'I presume that means you are quite unable to offer any solution.'

'Since the English police would not have informed Señor Drew, it has to be someone else.'

'That is logical. Who?'

'A friend who's in the police; a civilian who worked for them and does not feel bound by the rules.'

'You can suggest no more likely person?'

'I suppose it is possible Señor Howes learned the truth and told Señor Dawes.'

'Have you not in the past said no English policeman would pass on such information?'

'This would be different.'

'Why?'

'His daughter was killed. Circumstances can alter one's attitude to one's duties.'

'It is to be doubted any would alter yours . . . How would Howes have learned the truth and told Dawes?'

'He could be, or have been, a policeman.'

'Then you have made enquiries to learn if that is the case?'

'I had intended to do so the moment—'

'Clearly, the possibility had escaped you. You will ask him what is his profession or job; if he denies he is or has been a policeman, you will get in touch with whatever force he might have worked for and get them to confirm he was in a position to learn about Tyler.'

'I have your permission to do so, señor?'

'You amuse yourself by asking inane questions?'

'You recently made a point of reproaching me for not having received your permission to speak to a foreign force.'

'You are unable to appreciate that an order to do something is giving you permission to do it?'

'I just thought you might wish to be a little more specific. After all, if you order me to question X and I learn X lives abroad, do I travel abroad without asking for permission to make the journey?'

There was no answer, the line was dead.

Work was a virus multiplying at a lethal rate. Before Salas's first phone call, Alvarez had been faced by what some – not he – would have termed a reasonable amount of work; now, after the second call, he had to question Dawes, Howes, Higuero, possibly speak to the English police (and how was he to know whom to contact if Howes denied everything?), re-examine all the evidence, question the other women in Tyler's life (how to name them?), speak to Sophie Douste . . . And perhaps another dozen orders he had forgotten. His mind could no longer comprehend the future. He returned home.

THIRTEEN

'Do what?' asked the man in Vehicles, with angry disbelief. 'You're back, asking us to draw up another list and this time you can't be certain of the colour of the car, still don't know the letters of the registration number and the numbers might be wrong . . . Are you sure it was a car and not a donkey cart? It's bloody impossible!'

'The superior chief—'

'Can get stuffed.'

'I've no objection to that, but he'll raise trouble if you refuse.'

'Not half as much trouble as our boss will if the great Superior Chief Salas starts trying to tell him what we are to do.'

'So I say you refuse?'

'That's right.'

'You don't think it might be calmer for everyone if you say you'll try and then later on tell me you cannot succeed in providing a list which is short enough to make any investigation feasible?'

'We don't work like that.'

'Then you must be new to the job. Thanks for all your help,' Alvarez added sarcastically.

Some people were incapable of doing their job sensibly, saw trouble before it arose, felt no sense of shame at admitting incompetence. Still, the refusal did mean he was not going to be faced by hours of brain-destroying work, eliminating cars on a list a kilometre long.

He decided to question Howes, despite the long drive in the heat. If Howes was not a policeman, that would not only negate one possibility, it would annoy Salas, who seemed to believe himself omniscient.

He enjoyed an early *merienda* before he drove out of

Llueso, joined the autoroute just south of Mestara and after an easy drive reached Camp de Mar.

Kirsty opened the front door. 'You again!'

'I am afraid so, señora.' Face to face, he noted the irises of her eyes were large and an unusual dark shade of brown; they possessed a beauty that her other features did not.

'What is it this time?'

'I should like to speak to your husband again.'

'He's out.'

'Do you expect him to return soon?'

'There's no knowing.'

'Would you mind if I wait here rather than return to Llueso?'

'If you must.' She left the door open. 'I'm cooking. You'd better go out on to the patio.'

As he did as suggested, he wondered yet again what persuaded a man to marry the woman he married? Love, lust, pity, drink? Not even Salas, perhaps least of all he, could answer that question. On the pool patio, chairs, sun umbrellas, table and two air mattresses were set out as they had been on his previous visit. He moved a chair into full shade, sat.

The heat made the plunge pool enticing, even though he was no great lover of swimming. A hoopoe, in undulating flight, went from right to left, its plumage enhanced by the sunshine. Once it might have been killed and eaten. Conservation was restricted to the rich when there was little money, but much hunger. A single lantana beyond the pool was in full flower – the red and yellow of Spain. He could just hear the tapping sounds of a rock breaker at work; preparing to build one more house when the island was already overburdened. In the past, dynamite had been used to blast out rock where excavations had to be made, but there had been cases of structural damage to nearby buildings and swimming pools and explosives had been banned. Now the hammering could continue for weeks. Perhaps only the national and local fiestas had not been altered by the influx of foreigners. He hoped they never would be or the soul of the island would be in danger.

He awoke suddenly when Kirsty said, 'Well, are you?'

'I'm sorry, I was thinking.'

'Very deeply.'

'Am I what, señora?'

'Going to continue to wait here?'

'If that doesn't disturb you.'

'I should rather you . . .' She paused. 'My husband has just returned.'

He had heard nothing. As she went into the house, he reflected sadly that age robbed a man of hearing, sight, teeth, taste, and that most brutal loss of all . . .

Howes came out on to the patio. 'Good morning, Inspector. We seem to be very popular!' A lock of hair, escaping imprisonment, had fallen across his forehead. It required a filmic heroine to ease it back with her soft, loving hand. 'Has Kirsty offered you a drink, if it's not too early?'

Yet again, that incomprehensible qualification. 'One would be very welcome, señor.'

'Brandy with ice. Is that correct?'

'Thank you, yes.'

'Shan't be a moment.'

Several minutes later – after an argument inside between husband and wife, the words of which he had been unable to distinguish – Howes returned with two well filled glasses, put them down on the table, sat. He raised his glass. '*Salud!* . . . What brings you here today?'

'To ask if you're quite certain about what you told me.'

'What did I tell you?'

'The Drews had lunch with you here on Thursday.'

'I am quite certain.'

'You haven't had second thoughts?'

'I'm sticking with my first.' Howes drank, put his glass down on the table. 'Have you come all this way just to ask me if I've changed my memory?'

'No, señor. But I needed to make certain before I asked you what was your job in England?'

'A peculiar question.'

'But relevant.'

'I don't see how it can be.'

'Yet it is.'

Howes stared out at the trees beyond the patio. After a long pause, he said: 'Before I came here to live, I was a police constable.'

Had his appearance caused ribald comments from his companions and the public? Or had he been careful to look less theatrically handsome? 'You retired early?'

'I became choked with all the petty regulations imposed by the politicians; by the paperwork; by the public who criticized until they were in trouble. Kirsty inherited a cheerful amount of money from her aunt, we gave ourselves a holiday here, loved it and decided to quit England and move. A decision neither of us has ever regretted.'

'When you were still in England, I imagine you saw the Drews quite often?'

'As often as was feasible.'

'Despite the long journey?' Alvarez noted the brief expression of uncertainty.

'I like motoring.'

'The Drews live where?'

'Why ask me, not them?'

'To hear your answer.'

'I'm damned if I know where all this is leading.'

'Perhaps you will do so, when you tell me.'

'Sussex.'

'In which part?'

'What's it matter? . . . Apologies, Inspector, but I've had a bothering morning.'

'Sorry to hear that.' Alvarez noticed Kirsty was standing behind the nearest window, watching them. When he met her gaze, she turned away and disappeared from sight. 'Despite your many visits, you find it difficult to say whereabouts in Sussex they live?'

'Near Brighton.'

It was time for the sucker lie. 'I understood Señor Drew to tell me they lived in Lewes.'

'I'm getting muddled up with other friends. I told you, my mind's all over the place.'

'But you will clearly remember their house?'

'Yes.'

'Is it large?'

'Just ordinary size.'

'Old or new?'

'Neither one nor the other.'

'Señor Drew described it as old, with many beams.'

'What the hell are you getting at?' Howes spoke with nervous anger, immediately tried to erase the impression he might have given. 'Apologies again. I must be even more worried than I thought.'

'I don't believe you knew Señor and Señora Drew before you met them at the beginning of this month.'

'That's ridiculous.'

'When you say you visited them frequently, but have no idea where they live or what kind of house they live in?'

Howes picked up his glass, found it was empty.

'Can you explain what caused you to meet when you didn't know each other?'

'Whatever you say, we are old friends,' Howes repeated with weak insistence.

'Was it a common interest which brought you together? Yet how would you know there was one when you were strangers?'

Howes was sweating. He brought a handkerchief out of the pocket of his shorts, brushed his face and neck. 'It's like a bloody oven.'

Sweat from nervous tension, not heat. 'It think it was the tragic deaths of Irene Drew and Blaise Newcome, who were knocked down by a drunken driver.'

'I don't understand what you're talking about.' Howes picked up his glass. 'I need another.'

'I should prefer you to remain and answer my questions.'

He stood, went into the house. Alvarez again heard, without understanding the words, a conversation which was sufficiently excited to suggest argument.

Howes returned, sat, drank.

'Señor, for a time, the whereabouts of the driver of the fatal car was unknown. But after we were asked to help, it became certain where he was. You would have wanted to learn who and where that person was for many reasons. Using your friendship with a serving member of the police force, you did so. Has your wife been married before?'

'Yes.'

'Was her previous husband named Newcome?'

Howes finally muttered, 'Yes.'

'It was your stepson who was killed together with the Drews' daughter. You had a sad, bitter common interest with them.'

Howes drank until the glass was empty.

'The alibi you have been giving Señor Drew is false.'

'No.'

'You will know that deliberately to give false evidence is a serious offence.'

'That my wife lost her son, I, my stepson and they lost their daughter, doesn't begin to prove we would lie about seeing them. When I say they were here last Thursday, that is the truth.'

Alvarez stood.

'Can't you . . .?'

'Yes?'

'Forget it.'

He walked to the French windows, opened one, went into the house.

As Alvarez stepped out on to the road, a black estate, Kirsty Howes at the wheel, drove away.

A dark green car could, under certain conditions, look black; a black car would not seem to change colour whatever the conditions. Whatever Salas claimed, an estate car of one make did look very much like another. A stepfather could develop a similar degree of affection for his stepson as a father for his son. The alibi had cleared *Howes* as well as Drew. Yet he had noted the number and there was only one 3 in it. Could shock cause memory repetition?

He turned. A middle-aged man, short of stature but solidly built, dressed in hard-used working clothes, came across

the road. 'You're a private detective, aren't you?' he asked
in Mallorquin.

'Cuerpo,' Alvarez answered curtly.

'Guessed you was something like that.'

'I am nothing like that.' He was a qualified, highly trained
detective. 'Who are you?'

'Andrés.'

'Surname?'

'Ollers,' he answered, his manner subdued.

'Your identity card.'

'Why d'you want it?'

'Just show it.'

'I can't.'

'Why not?'

'It's at home.'

'You are required to have it on you at all times.'

'But I work in the gardens of foreigners and if I—'

'At all times,' Alvarez repeated, with the aggression of
authority about to strike. 'Not to do so is an offence.'

'I'll get it. Won't take five minutes on my Mobylette.'

Alvarez said nothing until satisfied he had gained revenge
for having been mistaken for a private detective. 'I'll forget
it this time.'

'That's very kind of you,' Ollers said obsequiously.

'What caused you to make so ridiculous a mistake?'

'Because you looked . . .' He did not finish.

Dolores had suggested before he left the house that his
shirt needed washing. 'Well?'

'Like someone of standing.'

'A private detective has none.'

'Of course not,' Ollers hastily agreed.

'Then explain why you were so stupid.'

'I've tried to.'

'One does not look at a man and think he is a private
detective unless one has reason to believe he might be.'

'I don't understand that.'

'I spoke very clearly.'

'But you said . . . I said . . .'

'You have said nothing that makes sense.' Alvarez

understood the satisfaction Salas felt when browbeating his
inspectors. 'What has happened to make you think it likely
a private detective would be here?'

'The Englishman.'

'Señor Howes?'

'If it's him what lives there.' He pointed at the house.

'Why would someone be interested in him?'

'She could want to know what he was doing.'

'Who is "she"?'

'His wife.'

'Why wouldn't she know what he was doing?'

'She was back in England and . . . He had a woman
here some time ago. I thought maybe his wife had learned
about it.'

'A friend providing company while she was away.'

'She was giving him company, all right.'

'Why do you say that?'

'Only had to look at her. Know what I mean?'

'No.'

'Maybe you ain't interested in women?'

'Your mistaken ideas will get you into deep trouble. Are
you trying to say she was attractive?'

'Never seen anyone like her before. Wasn't that she was
like one of them you see on the telly, all perfect. Look at
them and you can't believe they're real because you never
seen them on this island, more's the pity.'

'You've said what she wasn't like, now tell me what she
was like.'

'If you was ninety, you'd still be hoping.'

Alvarez decided to bring the conversation to an end. There
was little point in discussing what one would never be able to
enjoy. 'How long have you been working . . .' His imagination
suddenly went into overdrive. Not exactly beautiful, yet
instantly attracted a man's eager attention . . . 'Describe her.'

'I just done.'

'I want more details. What did you first notice about
her?'

'She was wearing something open and showing a bit of
tit.'

'Colour of hair?'

'Blonde.'

'Straight or curly?'

'More wavy.'

'Colour of eyes?'

'How would I know that?'

'A good figure?'

'Never seen one that gets you so . . . you know.'

'Did you hear her name?'

'When I was doing his garden and she was there, he was calling her something like "ma cherry" all the time.'

'Chérie. An endearment, not a name.'

'What's that supposed to mean?'

'What do you call your wife?'

'Ain't none of your business.'

'It was like saying *cariño*. You never heard him use an actual name?'

'Could have done maybe.'

'Can you remember what it was?'

Oller's expression suggested this was a difficult task. Eventually, he said: 'Could've been Susana.'

'Or Sophie?'

'Come to think about it, that's more like what it was.'

'Would you recognize her if you saw her again?'

'You don't see a prize dahlia and forget what it looks like.'

'Can't say I know what a dahlia is.'

'Because you can't accuse it of anything and lock it up.'

Alvarez smiled. 'I'll move on. You may have been of considerable help.'

'Ain't meaning to be.'

'We all do things we don't want to.' Reporting to Salas was one of them, Alvarez thought, as he drove away.

FOURTEEN

'Señor,' Alvarez said over the phone, 'I should like to report I have spoken again to Señor Howes.'

'And?' was Salas's sole comment.

'He admits he was a policeman before he retired.'

'Which was obvious.'

'Only if one—'

'There is not the time to listen to an endless, meandering and unintelligible comment from you. I have to drive to Palma by mid afternoon.'

Alvarez looked at his watch; it was a little after twelve.

'Has he confessed the alibi he gave Drew was falsified?'

'He admits Blaise Newcome was his stepson, but insists despite that he was, and is, not lying. Señor and Señora Drew were with them on Thursday, from the morning to the evening.'

'It seems you have carried out your interrogation with normal incompetence.'

'Señor, it might well be the truth and they were together then.'

'There are those, content to speak in meaningless clichés, who would answer, pigs might fly.'

'They do, in aeroplanes.'

'Then they are being flown, they are not flying.'

'Surely one says one is flying to Barcelona, not that one is being flown there?'

'There are many, of whom you are unfortunately one, who would.'

'In normal conversation, one often speaks colloquially—'

'Thereby showing either slackness or lack of education.'

'These days, if one does speak with formal correctness, one is likely to be regarded with amusement.'

'You regard me with amusement?'

'Of course not.'

'You have provided a prime example of the unthinking sloppiness of the speech of the common man.'

'I once heard the Duc de Paguera say—'

'Whenever you make a report, you confuse yourself and irritate the listener by discussing matters which have absolutely no connection with what the report is supposed to be about.'

'I should just like to make the point that colloquial speech can say in a few words what would take many times that number in formal speech.'

'Have you finished?'

'And you disparaged as a meaningless cliché the expression you used.'

'Purely as an example. You will ring off immediately, ring back in a quarter of an hour's time, by when you might be able to deliver a report which will consist only of matters germane.'

Alvarez replaced the receiver. He opened the bottom right-hand desk drawer, poured himself a reviving brandy.

He dialled, said he wished to speak to the superior chief.

'Señor, I have questioned Señor Howes and he insists Señor and Señora Drew were with them throughout the relevant time on Thursday. I asked him if he had been a policeman and he admitted this.'

'Do you intend to repeat everything you have already said?'

'I thought I would start at the beginning for the sake of clarity. Also, it sometimes helps both the speaker and the listener to go over something twice.'

'In your case, it confuses. I will ask you the questions; you will answer them, as shortly and concisely as you have the capacity to do. Was anything said when you interviewed Howes to suggest he was lying about the alibi?'

'No. The only thing was that he twice was having a row with his wife. Whether that carries any significance, I don't know.'

'A row about what?'

'I couldn't make out any of the words. But it was strange he should draw attention by arguing when I was there.'

'Your presence guarantees disturbance. Howes now admits he is the stepfather of Blaise Newcome?'

'Was.'

'Was what?'

'The stepfather. Blaise is unfortunately dead, so Howes isn't the stepfather, he was. In your previous call, you stressed the necessity of being factually and linguistically correct.'

'Which is why I now point out that it was not a call from me, it was you who phoned. Have you failed to make any significant progress in your investigations?'

'I am not certain.'

'The rest of us can be.'

'When I left Guillet—'

'Where?'

'As you may remember, señor, that is the name of the villa Howes is renting.'

'Anyone but you would have understood my question was intended to remind you to explain the relevance of what you were about to say.'

'What happened was I was about to get into my car after talking to Howes, when a man, Ollers, called out and came across, wanted to know if I was . . . if I was conducting a surveillance of the house. When I asked him why he should think that possible, he explained that when Señora Howes was away in England, Señor Howes had entertained a lady.'

'You are suggesting?'

'It was the entertainment a man likes to offer when his wife is away.'

'You are unable to accept it might be of the purest nature?'

Shades of what he had said to Ollers! 'I suppose that's just possible.'

'Your mind lives in darkness, as it is averse to light.'

'From her description, I doubt they had coffee and croissants.'

'You have met her?'

'No, señor.'

'Then your attitude reflects the regrettable desire to believe the worst.'

'Ollers said she possessed unusual qualities.'

'You have yet to explain who that man is.'

'He looks after several of the gardens of the villas and chalets that are rented out to tourists.'

'You no doubt meant to mention his occupation at the end of the report?'

'He saw her and describes her as a woman who would tempt a saint.'

'An ignorant description. A saint is beyond temptation.'

'She dresses very expensively.'

'Many women dress very expensively,' Salas said, calling his wife to mind. 'There is, by chance, some reason for telling me all this?'

'Do you remember the evidence of the staff at Es Teneres?'

'Do not judge my memory by yours.'

'They mentioned a French woman who for a time was so often in Tyler's company. I wonder if she is the woman Tyler saw.'

'Why should she be?'

'I have the feeling she might be.'

'Should that be classified as inspiration or hallucination?'

'A hunch.'

'You have provided not one simple fact to suggest the two ladies might be the same person.'

'The long, blonde, wavy hair.'

'Of which there has been no previous mention.'

'She is very attractive.'

'A meaningless description since attraction is in the eye of the beholder.'

'Señor, isn't that another cliché?'

'You mistakenly regard that remark as clever?'

'Wouldn't it have to be a great coincidence for two women of the same physical description to have contact, however slight, with persons connected with the case?'

'The description you have provided could apply to very many women.'

'But not when you add that she possesses qualities which instantly grip a man.'

'Qualities, of whatever nature, are incapable of physically gripping a man.'

'She wears unusual clothes.'

'Women do little else in this day and age.'

'They can be quite revealing.'

'Regrettably, that also is not unusual with the lower classes and those females who think themselves to be celebrities. Have you questioned her to learn if there is the slightest truth in your . . . hunch, did you call it?'

'I haven't had time to identify her or find out if she still lives here or has returned to France.'

'Why should she have done so?'

'She is very probably French.'

'I don't remember your telling me that. So this woman, who should not mistakenly be called a lady, a wraith in your mind, is in some way involved in the murder of Tyler even before her name is known? You strain the meaning of possible.'

'Señor, I have always understood that when conducting an investigation, one should consider everything and anything.'

'Which will explain why your career has shown so few successes.'

'I am convinced she is worth pursuing.'

'I am uninterested in your convictions.'

'If she did have fun with Señor Howes, she should at least surely be questioned.'

'You are now comparing adultery with fun?'

'For the adulterers.'

'Your mind descends even from the depths which it has long occupied. You will follow leads which are relevant, not those which attract you because of their nature. Have you anything else to report?'

'I don't think so.'

'A confused mind is certain of nothing,' were Salas's last words.

The sun was kind to Es Teneres. Shadows softened the sharp lines of the house, made it appear less stark, more welcoming.

Higuero was leaning his hands on the haft of a mattock, lightly dug into the soil, as he regarded a flowerbed in which bind weed was beginning to wind around miniature roses of many colours.

'Are you waiting for someone to come along and do your work for you?' Alvarez asked.

'Ain't no use you offering. Needs someone who knows what work is.'

'That bind weed is choking the roses.'

'Do I tell you how to do your job? Leave me to do mine.'

'Leaning on a mattock?'

'Where's the difference with you just standing there?'

'Let's move into the shade.'

'Why?'

'So I can ask some questions.'

'You ain't finished bothering people even after all this time?'

'And won't until I find out who shot Tyler.'

'He'll be forgotten long before you manage that.'

Alvarez crossed to one of the many oleander trees, stood in its shade. Higuero, to prove his independent spirit, did not join him for several minutes.

'Remember telling me about the women who used to come here?' Alvarez asked.

'No.'

'There was one in particular got you excited. Long, wavy, blonde hair, perfect figure, clothes that showed some of what's usually hidden.'

'What about her?'

'I need to talk to her.'

'Not heard it called that before.'

'You can help me find her.'

'Do your own dirty work.'

'I need to talk to her.'

'Wasting your time.'

'So you've suggested before. Do you know where she lives?'

'With her husband for some of the time, maybe.'

'Where do they both live?'

'No idea.'

'Tyler never mentioned her?'

'Him? Never spoke except to say what I was doing wrong or why had I left work early. Seemed to think that if he couldn't see me, I wasn't working.'

'Intelligent man. The car that nearly ran you down was a black estate, maybe an Astra, with the registration number 8533.'

'What about it?'

'Could it have been dark green?'

'Then I'd have said dark green.'

'You've never noted how sunlight can appear to alter colour?'

'Ain't never seen an orange grape.'

'Suppose I say the car could have been a Peugeöt?'

Higuero shrugged his shoulders.

'You'd swear on oath it was an Astra rather than a Peugeöt or Ford, even though it turned to go into the drive so quickly you didn't have time to get clear, were knocked off your Mobylette, and were shocked?'

'All I can say is, I reckoned it was an Astra.'

'You didn't read any of the letters in the registration number—'

'Nor would you have done if you'd just escaped being killed by a millimetre.'

'Consider things very carefully. Naturally, you tried to read the number to report the dangerous driving. What you won't have realized was how shocked you were and how shock can alter one's abilities.'

'What's all that supposed to be about?'

'I'm asking you to consider whether it's possible that the number you saw had only one three in it.'

'I tell as I remember.'

Memory was often fickle; it could be altered by hope, despair, fear, an unacknowledged connection . . . Ignore Higuero's stubborn refusal to admit he could be mistaken. There was reason, if small, to consider it might have been Howe's car. Yet what was the possibility that cars with threes in their registration numbers were owned by two

people who might be involved in the murder of Tyler? Yet
had he not used a similar coincidence to propose that the
two women with long blonde hair were one and the same?
One could not run with the rabbit and hunt with the hawk.

'Have you finished so as I can get on with me work?'
Higuero asked.

'Did you hear the shots last Thursday?'

'Working out here, I don't hear nothing from inside.'

'And you've no idea whether Tyler ever had a handgun.'

'You're asking?'

'Did he?'

'Yes.'

'Tell me how you know that.'

'I was going home when I found I'd forgot something,
so I came back. Heard shooting, had a look around and he
was with one of his women, firing at a row of flowerpots.
Missed the bloody lot. Every time the gun went off, she
cried out like he was trying to put his hand up her skirt.'

'Describe the gun. Was it an automatic or a revolver? Do
you know the difference?'

'Think I'm as ignorant as you lot? An automatic. Didn't
look big enough to do much harm, but likely it would ruin
a man's chances.'

'Where was he shooting?'

'Behind them oleanders.'

'Show me.'

They walked along the line of oleanders and round to an
area of untilled land, used for holding garden rubbish during
the summer until it was permissible to have a bonfire in
the autumn. At the end was a grass-covered mound, half a
metre high, of earth dug out when the foundations of the
garden shed had been laid. At the foot of the mound were
several broken flowerpots.

'Thought you said he didn't hit any?' Alvarez remarked.

'Probably kicked 'em when he finished missing 'em.'

Alvarez searched the ground and found twelve empty
cartridge cases. 'I need a bag to put these into. Have you
something?'

Higuero walked over to the shed, took a key out of his

pocket, opened the door and went inside; he returned with a crumpled plastic shopping bag.

Alvarez dropped the cases into the bag. Tyler had possessed a small automatic, had been shot by a small calibre automatic. Even Salas would have to accept the probability that it was the same gun. So the projected picture of the murderer having planned the murder, was probably incorrect.

'Where's the telephone directory?' Alvarez asked as he stepped into the dining room.

'Where it always is,' Jaime answered, as he put his glass down on the table.

'I can't see it.'

'What d'you want it for?'

'I need to find a French woman.'

Dolores appeared in the doorway of the kitchen, the parted strings of beads hanging down on either side of her. 'You disgrace the house by such an admission.'

'If you think—' Alvarez began.

'My thoughts are my own.'

'Occasionally,' Jaime muttered.

'You said something?'

He raised his glass and drank.

Alvarez spoke carefully. 'It is possible that a woman who is probably French can help me in my case. That is the only reason for wishing to get in touch with her.'

'And you will say that it is chance she is young, attractive and sufficiently naive to believe you are younger than you look.'

'I've no idea what her age is; she may be very attractive, or look like Matilde.'

'As if the poor woman is responsible for what she looks like! Men have no sympathy except for themselves. Lunch will be in fifteen minutes and you' – she looked directly at Jaime – 'will not refill your glass.'

'I've hardly drunk anything,' he complained.

'By your standards. By mine, there will already be many clouds in your mind.' She turned, swept into the kitchen.

Jaime watched Alvarez pour wine into his own glass,

pushed his glass across so that it could be refilled by someone else, thus obeying his wife's command.

'What's the meal?' Alvarez asked, as he replaced the bottle on the table.

'Can't say . . . This French woman – you've known her for a long time?'

'I've never met her.'

'Then why the fuss to find her address?'

'Didn't you hear me say she may be able to help me at work?'

'That was just to keep her quiet, wasn't it?' Jaime indicated the kitchen. 'Come on, there's no secrecy between friends.'

'She's more beautiful than any woman you've ever seen and she makes all the suggestions you're too bashful to propose.'

Jaime drank. 'There's times I feel like life's passed me by,' he said, louder than intended.

'It doesn't have to move quickly to do that,' Dolores called out from the kitchen.

FIFTEEN

Ca Na Sophie – misnamed since it should by tradition had been a nickname – was high in the urbanizacíon which climbed up the lower slopes of Puig Acro. From the house, there was a wide view across the flat land to Port Llueso, Llueso Bay and a slice of Palma Neuva. To any local, the property was proof that foreigners came to the island and were bewitched. Why else would one pay so much more for a home merely because it had a view and was without a garden in which could be grown food in times of trouble?

Alvarez braked to a halt and looked down the steep drive to the double garage. Motor down and there would be trouble turning, so he would have to reverse up to the road. When he was forced to reverse, the steering became traitorous and the car showed an eagerness to crunch into whatever was on either side. He turned off the engine, withdrew the keys, climbed out, used the remote to lock the doors. Slowly, he walked down, making use of the rope handrail to keep his balance.

By the side of the panelled front door was a brass plate reading MONSIEUR ET MADAME DOUSTE. He rang the bell, turned and looked up. The new road which was being cut out of the rock was still going to take many weeks to finish. Because of the cost of that work, because the mountain above increased in gradient, houses built along it would cost even more than those on the level on which he now was. Any downturn in the sale of properties to wealthy foreigners and the promoting firm would find themselves in debt with only a useless rock road as their asset.

'Yes?'

He turned to face a middle-aged woman whose appearance and dress marked her a local. 'Is Señora Douste here?'

'Yes.'

'I'd like to speak to her – and to Señor Douste.'

'Who are you?'

'Inspector Alvarez, Cuerpo.'

'Come to cause trouble?'

'I hope not.'

'I parked for five minutes in the village yesterday afternoon and received a fine of forty euros.'

'Blame the policia, not me.'

'You're all the same.'

Her manner marked female ignorance, not a declaration of Mallorquin independence.

'What do you want?'

'I'll explain to them.'

She sniffed loudly. 'Come in. They're through that room.' She pointed, walked away.

He crossed the hall, entered a sitting room furnished with taste and expense, and went out through the open French windows on to the patio. To the right, a sun blind was out and in its shade, lying on a patio recliner, was a sleeping man, whose noticeable stomach rippled to his breathing. To his left was a swimming pool, necessarily long and thin, in which a woman swam lazily, her long blonde hair trailing into a wedge shape.

She stopped swimming, stood, the water up to her waist. She wore a minimal bikini. 'You want something?' she asked in Spanish.

She was mocking him because she could judge he did not look at her and wonder what were her housekeeping abilities. 'Señora Douste?'

'No one else.'

'I am Inspector Alvarez of the Cuerpo General de Policia.'

'I've never met an inspector before.'

'The sign of a well spent life, señora.'

'You are very important?'

'Titles can be misleading.' She had a very shapely body, at least down to the water level, and despite the interruption of the water, he judged the perfection to continue. Her eyes were very blue, her nose chuckled, her lips were an invitation, her neck was graceful, yet the truth was, one saw greater beauty on the screen. But to accept that was to deny her the extra something. An erotic charm which could leave no man uninterested and, probably, no woman happy.

'You cannot answer what it is you want?'

'I should like to speak to Señor Douste.'

'But not to me?'

'I may wish also to ask you some questions.'

'Intimate ones?'

There was the sound of movement. Douste struggled into a sitting position. 'Who is it?' he demanded in French.

'A very important inspector,' she answered in the same language.

'What's he want? . . . Go inside and cover up.'

'Isn't it a bit late for that, sweetie? And I'm sure the inspector is uninterested in what I look like.' She reverted to Spanish. 'You are uninterested, aren't you, Inspector?'

'On duty, señora, I concentrate solely on my job.'

'How terribly boring for you. But perhaps your concentration sometimes wanders?'

'Only when there's reason for it to do so.'

'And there's no reason here?' she asked waspishly.

'What are you walking about?' Douste demanded.

'We're discussing what a detective needs to look at.'

'Never mind all that. Why is he here?'

'He hasn't said.'

'Just causing a damned nuisance like all the Spaniards.'

Alvarez said in French: 'I assure you, señor, I would not be troubling you unless there was good reason.'

Douste was annoyed by his mistake in assuming Alvarez could not speak French. He was a typical Parisian: 'I can't understand what you're trying to say.'

'Sweetie, you're making it seem you need a hearing aid.'

And a shot or two of Viagra, Alvarez silently added. It was difficult to judge the age difference, but it had to be considerable. While she enjoyed a body that was all smooth sweetness, Douste's resembled a badly shaped blancmange.

'Stop speaking Spanish so I can understand what's going on.'

'It's a compliment to him to speak his language.'

Doust's expression said to hell with compliments.

She climbed out of the pool, crossed to where Alvarez stood, continued to speak in Spanish. 'Do sit down.'

He settled on one of the patio chairs.

'Is there anything you would like which I can offer you?'

Standing there, beads of water sliding down her shapely figure, that was a question capable of being misunderstood.

'A drink, perhaps?'

'That would be very welcome, Señora.'

'What would you like? I can offer you most things, provided your taste is not too exotic.'

'I have simple tastes. A coñac with just ice.'

'Almost missionary.'

'Now what are you on about?' Douste demanded.

'I'm asking him what he would like to drink.'

'There was no need to do that.'

'You surely wouldn't want him to think you inhospitable?'

'I don't give a damn what he thinks.'

'You are in a mood, sweetie! We'll have to get you out of it.' She walked past Alvarez and across to a bell-push on the wall at the side of the French windows.

He tried not to watch her, but good intentions were like snow in the sunshine. She moved with the grace of a leopard.

The maid stepped out on to the patio.

'Irene, would you bring a coñac with ice for the inspector and champagne for the señor and me?' Sophie asked.

Irene returned indoors.

Sophie sat next to Alvarez. 'You mustn't judge my dear husband by his behaviour today. Unfortunately, he has just received a telephone call to say he unexpectedly has to return to Paris tomorrow for several days. It has annoyed him.'

'Who would not be annoyed in this weather?'

'Who indeed? Inspector – it's so boring to keep calling you that. What is your Christian name?'

'Enrique.'

'Are you going to go on speaking Spanish?' Douste demanded roughly in French.

'It's so much easier for the inspector and for you, since you say you cannot understand his French.' She turned.

'I'm becoming a little worried by you, Enrique.'

'I doubt that.'

'Every time you look at me, I see you wondering.'

He had hoped he hadn't been that obvious. 'I assure you, you are mistaken.'

'You look at me and wonder what sins I have committed and whether you will take me into captivity.'

'A sin is not a crime.'

'So I can sin and there's no need to worry what you will do to me?'

He did not answer.

Irene returned with a tray on which were two flutes, one glass, and a bottle of Bollinger in an ice bucket. She put the tray down on the table. Douste, with some puffing and blowing and a surge of his stomach, stood. He pulled the foil off the neck of the bottle, undid the wiring, gripped the cork with one hand, the base of the bottle with the other, and turned the bottle around the cork. He half filled the flutes, waited for the heads to subside, filled them, sat. Irene handed around the glasses, returned indoors.

Douste drank. He put the flute down on the table. 'Well?'

'Well what, sweetie?' she asked.

'Has he said why the hell he's here?'

Alvarez answered the question in French. 'Señor, you will have heard or read—'

'You think you can tell me what I have heard or read?'

'My apologies. Do you know about the murder of an Englishman, Señor Tyler, which occurred a week ago?'

'Yes.'

'I am in charge of the investigation and so am trying to find out as much about him as I can.'

'That fails to explain why you are here.'

'You may be able to help me.'

'You suggest I had any part in his murder?'

'No.'

'For your information, I was in Paris. So you are wasting your time and, more importantly, mine.'

'You knew Señor Tyler—'

'You are mistaken.'

'You were not at parties he gave at Es Teneres?'

'One. We left as soon as was socially acceptable.'

'Why was that?'

'The reason has nothing to do with you.'

'It may have.'

'If you continue to harass me, I shall write a letter of complaint to your superior.'

'Since I must continue asking questions and you seem to view this as harassment, would you like me to give you his name and address?'

She laughed. Douste muttered something.

'Perhaps, señor, you would tell me why you found his company objectionable?'

'I have no intention of doing so.'

'Sweetie,' she said, 'there's no point in making a mystery of it.' She continued in French when she spoke to Alvarez. 'At the one party we went to, my jealous husband thought Cyril was trying to inveigle me into seeing his etchings.'

Douste spoke angrily. 'His behaviour was outrageous.'

'Juvenile, but amusing.'

'Humiliating.'

'Why? He never made physical contact.'

'If he had, I'd have knocked him down.'

To visualize Douste's knocking a fit man down was difficult.

'Haven't I told you time and again, he was just joshing? Making amusing cocktail party conversation?'

Alvarez asked: 'You resented his behaviour, señor?'

'As any husband would.'

'Did you tell him so?'

'I made certain there was no further intercourse between my wife and him.'

'Very understandable, señor.' He was certain her blue eyes were laughing. 'You had spoken to him since then?'

'When we met in the village, as unfortunately happened, I took care to make him understand there would be no further contact. I will not acknowledge a man who lacks any notion of honourable behaviour.'

'He found dishonourable behaviour more fun,' she said.

'I wish you would not speak in that manner. A lady does not consider such a suggestion.'

'I wonder if Enrique would agree with you?'

'Who is Enrique?'

'The inspector.'

'I was not aware I had introduced him to you.'

'I decided there was no need for formality.'

'Not a decision for you to make. As you know, I do not agree with the casual use of Christian names.'

'Of course you don't, sweetie. You live in the nineteenth century.'

'I am happy to do so if that means I observe the manners of a gentleman.'

She turned to Alvarez. 'He doesn't appreciate the manners of a generation in the past. *Droit du seigneur* and all that.'

'A right for which there is little evidence.'

'It's a myth?'

'So it seems.'

'A young lady can no longer enjoy the thrill of wondering how she would have behaved?'

'Had there been recent contact between you and Tyler?'

'I wonder in what form you are using "contact"? Will it surprise you if I say there was?'

'No.'

'Speak French,' Douste demanded.

'It's so much quicker if I continue in Spanish and then if necessary tell you what he's saying. Otherwise he might be here so long I should have to offer him a bed.'

'You'll do no such thing.' Douste refilled his glass, ignored her empty one.

'Then we'll stick to Spanish.' She asked Alvarez: 'Do you know why I continued to see Cyril?'

'There could be many reasons.'

'What a cautious man. I always thought that girl whom Cyril employed was too interested and talkative.'

'She has told me nothing.'

'So was it the cook? Disapprovingly Desiccated, I've always called her.'

'She has never mentioned you.'

'You're not a very convincing liar, Enrique.'

'I have been told that before.'

'You didn't come here just to ask questions, did you?'

'What other reason could there be?'

'I think I'm beginning to dislike you.'

'Why?'

'For being so ungallant.'

'Why did you see Tyler when your husband made it obvious he disliked the man?'

'Because he forbade me to have anything to do with him.'

'When did you last see him?'

'Some time ago.'

'You haven't spoken to him recently?'

'He phoned not long before he died.'

'What did he want?'

'To see me again.'

'Did you?'

'No.'

'Even though your husband was away?'

'I became convinced that although the staff had taken my money to keep their silence, one of them was talking and caution became necessary. Then I heard from a very objectionable friend . . . Of no moment.'

'I would prefer to judge that.'

'I doubt your judgements. I suppose you are wondering if my husband learned the truth about my fun with Cyril and became so jealous, he shot him? Haven't you asked yourself if a lamb attacks a lion? . . . It was a pity. By refusing to meet Cyril, I lost the pleasure of disobeying my husband's specific edict. You know all about that kind of pleasure, don't you?'

'As a serving officer, I obey the rules.'

'Which I hope you make up to suit yourself?'

'What the devil is it all about now?' Douste asked angrily. He refilled his glass, again ignored hers.

'I'm asking him why he asks so many questions,' she answered, 'and he's explaining that the police need to know everything. But as I said, a lady can't tell all her little secrets and lose the pleasure they provide.'

'How much longer is this going to go on?'

She switched to Spanish. 'Well?'

'I'll leave when you tell me how well you knew Señor Howes,' Alvarez answered.

'I'm not certain.'

'It does seem unlikely you could ever have bothered to know him, but I believe you visited his house more than once when his wife was in England.'

She laughed.

'Is that an admission?'

'Make of it what you will, sweet Enrique.'

He stood.

'You're going?'

'Yes.'

'Because my husband has said you must?'

Because he was fed up with being auditioned by a woman whom, he was certain, would eventually reject him with scornful amusement. He spoke to Douste. 'I should like to thank you for your kind patience.' He walked toward the French doors.

'You may not be a good liar, Enrique, but you are an accomplished hypocrite,' she called out.

Jaime pushed across the bottle of Soberano. Alvarez poured himself a generous measure, added three cubes of ice.

'What kind of a day has it been for you?' Jaime asked casually.

'Interesting, but frustrating.'

'Are you on about work or women?'

'Not much difference in this case.'

'You've some funny ideas.'

'You have to work hard to get anywhere with either.'

'Wouldn't know these days.'

'What wouldn't you know?' came the call from the kitchen.

'What day it is,' Jaime replied, surprising Alvarez with his quickness of thought.

'What does it matter what day it is?' Dolores appeared through the bead curtain.

'Just wondering.'

'Perhaps you were thinking when you would mend the fan in the kitchen?'

'There won't be time before grub tonight . . .'

'Grub! *Grub?* You consider that is what I serve after working for hours in a kitchen which is hotter than the racks on which saints were roasted because my husband will not mend the fan? Then there is no reason for me to continue to cook.'

'I didn't mean it like that. It's just—'

'Insulting.'

'It's a common word for food.'

'Eaten by people with common tastes.'

Jaime reached across the table for the bottle.

'You have had enough,' she said sharply.

'I've hardly had any.'

'And will continue to have hardly any. Even if I am capable of only cooking "grub", I do not intend to serve it to someone who cannot decide from which of the two plates to eat.' She retired into the kitchen.

'Doesn't matter what you say,' Jaime muttered, 'always takes it the wrong way.'

'Which occasionally can be the right way.' Alvarez drank.

'What's that supposed to mean?'

'I was thinking of a woman I met earlier.'

'Who frustrated you?'

'It was the impossibility which was frustrating.'

'Can you ever understand yourself? . . . Move a little to your right.'

'Why?'

'She won't be able to see me if she looks out.'

Alvarez quietly moved his chair. Jaime even more carefully poured himself another brandy. He drank. 'What's with this woman you're talking about? Real smart looking? Makes the nerves tingle?'

'Pleasant, but no great modern beauty.'

'But you still had a try and failed?'

'My problem was that I had to struggle to fail.'

'Have you been boozing all afternoon?'

'One coñac.'

'In a litre glass.'

'Have you ever met a woman who sent your mind off into a whirlpool?'

'Thought you said she was no oil painting?'

'I doubt there's an artist can paint her charms.' He swore.

'Now what?'

'I've just remembered there's someone I should have questioned before returning home.'

'Wouldn't have done you much good unless you made more sense than you are now.'

SIXTEEN

Alvarez had settled behind his desk, regained his breath after the climb up the stairs, and was considering whether to work when the phone rang.

'The superior chief will speak to you.'

He waited.

'I have been expecting to have a report from you,' Salas said. 'Unfortunately, you give no heed to the words "I cannot wait and yet not be tired by waiting."'

'The fact is, señor, I have been very busy.'

'Doing what, since it is unlikely to have been work?'

'I set out to question Señor Howes, Señor Douste and Higuero.'

'Howes admits his evidence concerning the alibi was false?'

'I'm afraid he still does not.'

'It was remiss of me to reject the idea of having Inspector Malberti conduct the examination.'

'However, I have learned something of great importance.'

'Surprising.'

'Tyler was a secret Wyatt Earp.'

'Would you explain what you are talking about – if, indeed, you know?'

'Higuero returned to Es Teneres after work one evening in order to retrieve something he had forgotten to collect. He heard shooting and checked to see what was going on. At the end of the property, Tyler was imitating Earp.'

'Now explain what that means.'

'You haven't read about Earp, señor?'

'Is there any reason why I should have done?'

'He was one of the greatest lawmen in the Wild West. He was at the battle of the O.K. Corral.'

'How can a gunman have the slightest connection with what Higuero saw?'

'Tyler was with one of his women. He was wearing a

gun in a holster and was repeatedly pulling the gun out and firing at some old clay pots. He couldn't hit any of them and ended up smashing them by kicking.'

'The gardener must have a perverse sense of humour and finds it amusing to feed nonsense to someone of great naivety.'

'There is reason to believe him.'

'There is greater reason not to believe him. The gun which killed Tyler was an automatic. The murdering lawmen, wrongly perceived by some as heroes, used revolvers.'

'You do know something about them, then.'

'As befits my position, I have knowledge of many things even though I have no interest in them.'

'Then I am surprised you did not know about Wyatt Earp.'

'I have no wish for your opinion. It has not occurred to you that Higuero was making a fool of you?'

'He showed me where the shooting had taken place. There were several shell cases on the ground and a number of broken pots. I have sent the cases to the laboratory for examination. My judgement is that they are—'

'I prefer to wait for a judgement of some quality. You have not heard from the laboratory?'

'Not yet.'

'Then you can refrain from any further conjectures which can only prove to be false. As I understand it, you have only just been informed of this unlikely story?'

'Men play at being Wild West heroes in America, señor.'

'Tyler was an Englishman.'

'I understand that there, men shoot each other with paint balls.'

'If there can be any truth in that, then it is further evidence of the juvenile nature of the Anglo-American psyche. Will you now cease wasting my time and answer the question?'

'Which was what, señor?'

'Why have you only just reported this to me? Perhaps the answer is too self-evident to need you to give it. You had not questioned Higuero before, despite my ordering you to do so many days ago.'

'I had a word with him, immediately. He denied any knowledge of a gun. Yet when I questioned him again, he

told me about the shooting incident and couldn't understand why I was so annoyed he hadn't mentioned it before.
I fear he is not very intelligent.'

'If that is your judgement, then he must be virtually
witless.'

'I have learned something more. The identity of Madame
Douste.'

'You expect me to appreciate the importance of this when
I have not heard the lady's name before and you have not
seen fit to explain who she is?'

'I thought I had mentioned her to you on previous occasions, señor?'

'You thought incorrectly.'

'She is the blonde who has turned up from time to time.'

'Am I to presume you are referring to the woman whom
you have on occasion mentioned in obnoxious terms?'

'I think even you would find her . . .' He stopped quickly.

'What?'

'Unusual.'

'In what manner?'

'Her assets are basic.'

'That is supposed to convey something meaningful?'

'I thought it might.'

'Typical! You expect to be understood when your words
are meaningless. Why is she of any importance to this case?'

'She virtually admitted that she did go down with Tyler.'

'Down where?'

'It's an expression. Perhaps you are not conversant with
it?'

'Because it is of a prurient nature?'

'She and Tyler were very close.'

'Explain yourself.'

'They were having an affair.'

'Which explains your interest in her.'

'The fact supports the possibility of jealousy being the
motive for the murder.'

'You are proposing that this woman's husband shot Tyler?'

'That's doubtful. He's considerably older than she, over-
weight and slothful, and there's no reason to think he knew

what she was up to. But Tyler did not restrict himself to
one woman. A man of his nature never does because variety
and pursuit afford as much pleasure as—'

'Cease exposing your louche interests.'

'Her affair has to point to another husband having learned
what was going on and being sufficiently jealous to have
good reason to commit murder.'

'No reason can condone murder.'

'If your wife was—'

'Enough!'

'If my wife was having an affair with another man—'

'Are you married?'

'No, señor.'

'Then your observations are not only unnecessary, they
are also of no consequence. Do you have the names of other
women whom this man has debauched?'

'No. But it is certain he was very active.'

'So it is pure surmise when you say that the husband of
one of these unknown women is involved?'

'I suppose you could say that. But if one thinks about it—'

'Which you delight in doing. You will restrict your efforts
to uncovering the evidence which will prove Tyler was
murdered because he had been driving the car which killed
the couple in England. Is that clear?'

'Only—'

'Is. That. Clear?'

Alvarez said it was. He listened to a lecture on the duty
of an inferior to accept the orders of his superior without
question. The call finally came to an end. He hesitated, but
only briefly, before he opened the bottom right-hand drawer
of his desk.

Howes was wearing a blazer with a crest on the breast
pocket, white shirt, light fawn cotton trousers with sharp
creases, white socks and white loafers. Perhaps, Alvarez
thought, he really did see himself in an ancient film. 'Good
morning, señor.'

'Not again?'

'I fear so.'

'If you want to speak to Kirsty, I'm afraid she's out.'

'I think you may find reason to be grateful for that.'

'What . . . How d'you mean?'

'If I might enter?'

'I . . . I was just about to go out myself.'

'I fear you will have to delay your departure.'

'You can't make me stay here.'

'That is true. But our law allows me to make certain you are charged with refusing to assist me and so can be restrained somewhere less pleasant.'

'Oh, God! I wish she hadn't persuaded me. I told her it was a crazy idea.'

'What was this crazy idea?'

He hesitated. 'To sell up at home and live here.'

'Señor, I have been working long hours and my legs are tired. Might we go inside and sit?'

'Why?'

'I need to ask you some questions.'

'I've told you everything I can.'

'I have learned more facts which necessitate further answers from you. May I enter?'

Reluctantly, Howes led the way inside, but did not go through to the patio, slumped down on one of the chairs. 'We'd better wait until Kirsty returns.'

'You still do not understand what I meant when I said it would be better for you if she were not here?'

'No.'

He needed his wife's strength to buttress his weakness, even though he must fear what she might learn. 'You have assured me Señor and Señora Drew were here for much of Thursday, the fourteenth.'

'Yes.'

'And your wife was also here.'

'Yes.'

'She had not returned to England for a while?'

'She was here. How can I make you understand?'

'By telling me the truth.'

'I need a drink.' Howes stood.

'Sit down.'

He looked at the French windows as if hoping for the timely arrival of his wife, sat.

'Does your wife return to England from time to time?'

'To see a close relative.'

'And then you are here on your own?'

'Yes.'

'But not always?'

'What . . . what are you getting at?'

'Do you not sometimes have a visitor when your wife is away?'

'No.'

'You have no friends who drop in to cheer you up if you're feeling slightly lonely?'

'I thought . . .' He stopped.

'I was referring to Sophie?'

After a moment of panic, he asked: 'Who?' in a croaky voice.

'Sophie Douste.'

'I don't know anyone of that name.'

'You surprise me. She told me you were a close friend of hers.'

Howes rushed out of the room.

Alvarez stared through the window at the pool, the trees, a passing seagull. Nothing was isolated – every action carried consequences; pleasure was trailed by pain.

Howes returned, a glass in a shaking hand causing the whisky to ripple. He sat, drank. 'She . . . she's just a friend. The thing is . . . Kirsty doesn't like her.'

'Few wives would.'

'We just meet to enjoy each other's company.'

'Very understandable.'

'We talk.'

'Before, during or after?'

'I tell you, it wasn't like that.' He drained the glass.

'I have to know the truth. Were Señor and Señora Drew here that Thursday?'

'Yes,' Howes finally answered.

'I'm afraid I don't believe you and will have to find out

the truth. Do you understand what will happen if you continue to lie?'

'I am not lying.'

'Because I must know if I am right, I will have to ask many more questions and when your wife learns this, I believe she will wish to be present. Unfortunately, your relationship with Madame Douste will be mentioned.'

'You . . . you're going to tell Kirsty about her?'

'I naturally will be as tactful as possible, but regrettably it is difficult to believe she will accept with equanimity the presence of so attractive a woman in her absence.'

'You can't!'

'I have no option.'

'But Kirsty can . . . She'll think I was having an affair.'

'It would seem to her to be a logical conclusion.'

'Don't you understand what that would mean? It's her house. She's so . . . so illiberal. She won't listen to me. She might even throw me out. I have a pension, but it's only small. You mustn't let her know!'

'Until I am convinced of what is the truth, I don't think I have any option but to question you both together.'

Howes picked up his glass, left the room, returned, sat, drank. 'If I tell you . . .'

'Tell me what happened that day, will I forego any mention of Sophie in front of your wife? Since to do that would cost you both such distress, it is something I am very reluctant to do. I suppose it might be possible to withhold any mention of Sophie's visits here – provided I am convinced to do so would have no direct adverse consequence.'

'You swear?'

'I can promise nothing.'

'You said you wouldn't mention her.'

'Unless you force me to do so.'

'What do you want to know?' Howes asked, his voice shaky.

'Were the Drews here that Thursday?'

He twice started to speak, stopped; the third time, he said: 'No.'

'They asked you to give them a false alibi?'

He nodded.

'Earlier, you said something was a crazy idea and I don't think it was referring to your coming here to live. What was the idea?'

'She said it would help.'

'Who and what?'

'Sandra said it had worked in South Africa. She talked about how making criminals face their victims and apologize helped the victims. The confession of guilt and acknowledgement of the harm caused brought relief. If Tyler would admit he had been driving the car which had knocked down Irene and Blaise, would apologize for the terrible hurt he had caused, we would find some relief from grief. Tim thought that was nonsense, as I did. A drunken man kills your stepson and the fact he says he's sorry can make the tragedy any more bearable . . .'

'Did you see Tyler?'

'We drove to his place, knocked on the front door and a maid opened it. We said we wanted to speak to him and gave our names. She told us he refused to see us and we'd better clear off or there'd be trouble.'

'You went back another time?'

'What was the use? A man like him was never going to confess.'

'Why have you stayed on in Mallorca?'

'I suppose it sounds terrible, but we'd booked for three weeks. Some holiday!'

'Thank you for telling me this.'

'You think I'd have done so if you hadn't blackmailed me into it?'

'I hope you don't mean that.'

'Too goddamn right I do!'

'I had to know the truth.'

Alvarez wondered, Did one always have to know the truth? It could be so very much more painful for people than a lie.

SEVENTEEN

He entered the dining room. Jaime sat at the table, a glass in front of him. Isabel and Juan were arguing, Dolores was laying the table.

'The traffic was so bad, I was afraid I was going to be late,' Alvarez said.

Dolores placed the last glass on the table, ordered the children to be quiet, said he was too late to have a drink before the meal, went into the kitchen. Alvarez was about to pour himself a drink to prove her wrong, when she re-appeared. 'There have been so many interruptions because of phone calls for you, Enrique, I have not had the time to prepare the meal properly.'

'I'm as sure it will, as always, be perfection.'

'As my mother used to say, "A man's tongue is a weathervane, indicating in which direction he thinks the wind will blow." That ill-mannered man who is your superior officer rang three times, rudely demanding to know where you were and why couldn't I tell him. I replied each time, with a politeness foreign to any Madrileño, that I did not have the wish or opportunity to interest myself in your comings and goings. There was also a call from a woman. She said she had been expecting to hear from you.'

'Who was she?'

'I did not wish to know.'

'She didn't give a name?'

'No.'

'You've no idea who she might have been?'

'She is a foreigner since her Castilian accent is bad and she does not speak Mallorquin.'

'I can't think of any lady who can be expecting me to get in touch with her . . .'

'But,' Jaime said, 'I bet there are a dozen *women* you can name.'

'What's the difference between a lady and a woman?'
Juan asked.

'You will take no notice of your father when he talks
like that,' Dolores said sharply.

'Talks like what?'

'In a manner unsuited to your young ears.'

'Like when you said to father, she sounded like one of
uncle's . . . What was it?'

'I do not remember.'

'One of uncle's foreign tarts,' Isabel said.

'How dare you speak such words!'

'But you—'

'You are making it up.'

'No, I am not. And—'

'Do you wish to make me very annoyed?'

Isabel shook her head, but her expression was defiant.

'I apologize for my children's behaviour,' Dolores said,
without sounding in the least apologetic. 'Sadly, their minds
have been sculpted by their father's manners.'

'Why bring me into it?' Jaime asked plaintively.

'That you need to ask shows your unfortunate influence.'
She swept back into the kitchen.

'She did say that,' Isabel said.

'Be quiet,' Jaime muttered.

'What is a tart?'

'I can tell you,' Juan answered with pride.

'If you two don't shut up . . .'

Jaime's threat was not completed. The phone rang several
times.

'Will someone find the energy to think of answering?'
Dolores called out.

'Won't be for me,' Jaime said. He picked up his glass.

'It's for uncle,' Isabel said. 'From her . . . What's she
called?'

Alvarez hurriedly stood and made his way into the
entrada, where the telephone stood on a small corner shelf.
He picked up the receiver. 'Yes?'

'Have you forgotten what I told you?'

'Who's speaking?'

The call ended.

He replaced the receiver, stared at the telephone. He told himself he had not recognized the voice and there was no way of identifying her, so forget the incident. What had he forgotten? That her husband would be in Paris? What absurdity to think Sophie would have bothered to phone him in so provocative a manner.

He returned to the dining room.

Dolores stepped through the bead curtain. 'Are you all right?'

He nodded.

'Looks like the bank manager's told him he's a thousand euros overdrawn,' Jaime said.

'Perhaps it was one of his—' Juan began.

'You wish to spend the next day living on bread and water?' Dolores snapped. Her tone changed and became solicitous. As always, if she believed one of the family might be in trouble, she rushed to help; her tongue might be sharp, but her touch was soft. 'Enrique, was that bad news?'

'I don't know.' He picked up the bottle and refilled his glass.

'Was that your absurd superior chief causing still more trouble?'

'No.'

'Has something happened to upset you?'

He needed to explain his air of bewilderment. 'It's just one of the cabos reporting something very unusual.'

'You have to leave immediately?'

'No.'

'Then I will serve the meal. I have prepared *Morula a la Riverina*. Eat well and you will feel better.'

His mind was not on the coming meal.

He settled behind his desk and hurriedly lit a cigarette before he remembered he had promised himself not to smoke before midday.

The phone rang.

'It is now nine twenty,' Salas's secretary said reprovingly.

He looked at his watch. She was correct.

'I phoned at nine and there was no answer.'

That was probably when he had finished his second slice of *coca*. 'I was checking emails, señorita.'

'The superior chief will speak to you.'

What a way to start the day!

'I have been expecting to hear from you, Alvarez, but where you are concerned, commendable expectations are seldom fulfilled,' Salas said curtly.

'I have been gathering as much evidence as possible, señor, in order to make a comprehensive report. Do you remember telling me I was wasting my time questioning Madame Douste?'

'And forbidding you to do so.'

'It hasn't been time wasted, señor.'

'Are you admitting you have disregarded my order?'

'I thought it very advisable to speak to her. And by doing so, I learned she was very friendly with Señor Howes.'

'Why is that of any importance?'

'Howes is married to a woman with considerably more money than he has, is something of a Tarta, very narrow-minded, and would throw him out of her house if she learned about it.'

'So far, you might be reporting in Tartarian for all I have understood.'

'They were very friendly.'

'Must you keep repeating yourself?'

'Perhaps you do not understand?'

'I have just expressed myself on that point.'

'"Very friendly" has a secondary meaning.'

'Neither word is in the least ambiguous.'

'It means they were having fun together.'

'Friendship promotes pleasure.'

'In this instance, it promoted an intimate pleasure.'

'You are indulging in your reprehensible urge to find impurity in every relationship?'

'She admits they were lovers.'

'An admission which no doubt gives you satisfaction, but is of no account to others.'

'When I explained to Señor Howes that unless he finally told me the truth, there would have to be a more intensive investigation into his life and this must mean his wife would learn what he had been up to, he confessed to avoid her knowing.'

'Perhaps you would take the trouble to explain what was the truth to which he confessed?'

'But that's surely obvious?'

'What is obvious to you is often mercifully hidden from others. Kindly try to give a comprehensible report.'

'Señor Howes admits that Señor and Señora Drew were not with them that Thursday. So neither couple have an alibi. Further, Señor Howes explained why they had come to the island. The two wives thought that if Tyler would admit he had been driving the car which killed their children, they would gain relief from their mental pain . . . I agree with the two husbands that had Tyler confessed – of course, he refused even to talk to them – there would have been very little relief gained, but there are people who think differently from me.'

'Which is a consoling thought.'

'So you see, had I not set out to meet Madame Douste, we would not have determined that the alibi was false.'

'You may possibly remember that the reason you gave me for wishing to identify her was you thought she might be able to name a husband who had learned his wife had betrayed him with Tyler. Has she provided many names?'

'Not really.'

'Has she provided any?'

'No, señor.'

'As I said at the time, it was a ridiculous proposition and was not to be pursued.'

'But we weren't getting anywhere.'

'You were not.'

'It seemed right to try anything. After all, there could have been pillow talk with a man who was of a character to boast about his—'

'You will not pursue the matter.'

'If I hadn't identified and talked to her, I would not have

been able to persuade Señor Howes to admit the alibi was false.'

'Persuading him in a manner alien to that required of a member of the Cuerpo.'

'I don't think you can say that.'

'I have just done so.'

'We know that Señor Drew—'

'Are you naming him the murderer?'

'I've always said that's unlikely, even if grief can change character, and there's little, if any, hard evidence against him. No question, he had a very strong motive, but there's no evidence he was at Es Teneres when Tyler was shot.'

'Was he not seen leaving there? Why would he have been driving so dangerously except to escape the murder scene?'

'We can't prove it was his car.'

'A false alibi presupposes a crime.'

'But will we be able to prove its falsity?'

'Have you not spent a considerable time saying, with much self-congratulation, that you have succeeded in doing so?'

'Señora Howes was not present. Had she been, he might well not have found the courage to deny the falsity of his evidence. Since her return home, he may have managed to confess his relationship with Madame Douste in such a manner as to hide the truth and not enrage his wife to the point of throwing him out of her life. Without the threat of exposing his affair to his wife, he can deny everything he said to me.'

'In other words, the matter has been handled incompetently.'

'At least we do know Tyler possessed a small calibre automatic.'

'What is the laboratory's report on the cartridge cases?'

'I haven't been able to check.'

'Too busy disobeying my orders. You will find out immediately whether or not the cases you sent might have come from the same kind of gun as killed Tyler. You will try far more energetically to find proof that the car seen leaving Es Teneres was Drew's car, driven by him. You will re-examine all the evidence, determine if, as is most likely, you have ignored something that is of great importance. I expect to hear from you regarding all these matters in the near future.' He did not bother to say goodbye.

Work, work, work. Endless toil drained a man's being. Alvarez lifted the receiver and dialled.

'Inspector Alvarez here . . .'

'It's never anyone else these days.'

'Superior Chief Salas wants to know whether you have been able to check the cartridge cases I sent you?'

'Yes.'

'Have you come to any conclusion?'

'They are from an automatic of the same calibre as the bullets which killed Tyler.'

'The gun which fired them was the same one used to kill him?'

'Anything more than I have said is pure conjecture.'

'But reasonable conjecture?'

'You decide what's reasonable.'

Alvarez leaned back in his chair, lifted his feet up on to the desk. Nothing had been learned to prove – as opposed to suggest – it had been Drew's car which had driven furiously away from Es Teneres immediately after Tyler's murder. Drew had expressed his disbelief that an admission of guilt from Tyler would have brought any relief to him. Murder held the harsh, bitter satisfaction of knowing his daughter had been revenged. And as Salas had remarked, if there was no guilt, there was no need to set up a false alibi.

Why, he asked himself, was he so reluctant to accept Drew's guilt when known facts pointed to it? Who else would have been driving his car?

He suddenly remembered being told that Tyler would never go household shopping, would not be seen carrying a plastic shopping bag. That scrumpled up receipt found under Tyler's desk. He had the vague notion that after it had been photographed several times beneath the desk, he had picked it up in order to put it in a small exhibition bag, only to find he had no such bags with him . . . He checked the pockets of his trousers and was not all that surprised to find the receipt. He smoothed it out. Dated the 13th of August. He skimmed down the purchases, stopped when he came to two items. Would a man have bought products peculiar to a woman's needs? Wouldn't he be embarrassed to do so, wouldn't she prefer to make the purchases herself? Why would a husband have possession of the receipt for purchases made by his wife? . . .

Yet Higuero had again and again identified the driver of the car as a man.

EIGHTEEN

The swimming pool at Aparthotel Vora La Mer appeared to be holding an even greater number of shouting children and fatigued parents than before. Alvarez walked around it, as far away as possible, yet still was splashed. Childhood today, he thought sadly and a touch bitterly, was so very different from what he had known. By eight, he had worked in the fields to help his father planting, hoeing, irrigating, cropping. School was for those who could afford the fees. He had been lucky. A close pal had attended the local school run by nuns and he had returned each day and repeated the lessons to him. It had surprised his parents to discover he could read. By ten, he had been responsible for much of the care of their few animals as well as being required to work harder and longer on the land. By fifteen, he had travelled no further afield than Inca. The foreigners, mostly English, who had visited the part of the island where he had then lived, had been regarded with unease; when, occasionally, they had handed him a few coins, with awed unease. Once, an elderly Englishwoman, noting the state of the clothes he had been wearing, had given him a ten-peseta note and his father had taken this from him, explaining they needed the food it would buy. It had needed time to overcome his resentment at the loss of an endless supply of sweets.

He banged into a man in bathing trunks, apologized, realized he had been so deep in reverie, he had gone almost around the pool and the attendant was regarding him with watchful curiosity. He walked down to the Drews' apartment, knocked. There was a call to enter.

Husband and wife were seated at the small table in the main room; on the table were glasses, an opened bottle of cava with water-beaded surface, and a bowl of crisps.

'I apologize for troubling you yet again,' he said.

'It's no bother.'

Their lack of surprise said he had been expected. Howes had phoned them to explain what had happened.

'Do sit down. And will you have some cava?'

'Thank you, no.'

'Whisky, brandy?'

'May I have a coñac, please, with just ice?'

Drew went into the compact kitchen. Sandra initiated a conversation about the beauty of the mountains which they had explored by car and asked why did he think so few visitors enjoy visiting them?

Drew returned with a well filled glass, handed this to Alvarez, sat. 'What is the problem this time?' He tried to speak lightly, failed.

'Has Señor Howes spoken to you recently?'

Drew hesitated, finally said: 'Not for a couple of days.'

'Then you do not know I had reason to ask him again about the alibi he and the señora had provided you. I persuaded him finally to speak the truth. You are not old friends. The first time you will have seen each other was at the inquest in England when, no doubt, you only had the briefest acquaintance. So when you met here on the island, it was very much as strangers.'

Sandra muttered something, her expression was despairing.

'And you were not at their house at any time that Thursday.'

Drew said nothing. The shouts and laughter from the pool became an ironic background noise.

'Señor, on that Thursday afternoon, you were driving the car which left Es Teneres at excessive speed and caused the gardener, Higuero, to fall off his Mobylette.'

'I was not.'

'Did you know Tyler had a small automatic?'

'How could I?'

'Did you mean to scare him and he thought to defend himself? If so—'

'He killed our daughter.'

'However much one may think he deserved to die, modern law does not allow a life for a life.'

'He was so rich he bought himself out of trouble.'

'You must know that money cannot cover guilt in England, just as it cannot in Spain. He was not charged with the death of your daughter and the son of Señora Howes because the evidence needed to convict him might be on the car and that was missing. When it was finally found, it had been repaired, making identification of it as the fatal car impossible until further tests were carried out. Unfortunately, he was murdered before these could be done.'

Drew, his voice strained, said: 'He was so scared, I thought he was going to kill me.'

'No!' she cried out.

Drew picked up his glass and drained it.

'No, please no,' she said, now speaking in a low, pleading voice.

He reached his free hand across and briefly took hold of one of hers. 'As the inspector has suggested, I have been a blind fool to go on denying the truth. When we learned Tyler's name, we went to his house to ask him to confess. The maid told us he wouldn't speak to us and to clear off. We had to leave. Later, I determined to face him, make him understand what a worthless bastard he was. I drove to his house. The front door wasn't locked so I walked straight in. There were sounds from a room and I went into the library. Tyler was sitting behind the desk. I went round that and started telling him why I was there. He became scared, opened one of the drawers, pulled out a small gun, aimed it at me and ordered me out of the house. He was in such a blue funk, I was afraid he'd fire by mistake, so I lunged forward and grabbed his wrist, twisted it. The gun went off twice. He collapsed, fell over with the chair. I panicked, lacked the courage to call for medical help, fled.'

Sandra was crying silently, her head fallen forward. Tears dropped on to the table.

'So now I suppose you arrest me?'

'Further enquiries will have to be made, to confirm it was an accidental death despite your admission you went to the house in an aggressive mood. In the meantime, you will give me your passport and you will agree not to leave Port Llueso.'

Drew stood, left the room.

She raised her head. 'You don't know what it was like. You can't understand. You don't care . . .'

'Señora, I can try to imagine what it was like for you and the señor, but bitter sorrow can only be known for its brutality by those who experience it.' As he once had. 'I am very sorry for both of you, but I have to obey the law and the law does not allow sympathy.'

Drew returned and handed over his passport. Alvarez stood, wished he could say something helpful and couldn't, left the apartment. There were fewer people in the pool now that many were having lunch, but the shouting and splashing continued. In front of him happiness; behind him, fear. Life.

Back in his office, he rang Palma.

'Yes?'

'I should like to speak to Señor Salas, señorita. It is Inspector Alvarez speaking.'

'The superior chief is not here.'

'Gone to an early lunch?'

'He is at a meeting. He does not stop for an early lunch, he works until all work is finished. Why do you want to speak to him?'

'To tell him Señor Drew admits the alibi was false and that he was present at Tyler's death.'

'Very well.'

He said goodbye, replaced the receiver, checked the time. He needed to hurry home for pre-lunch drinks.

He had finished the first brandy when the telephone rang. 'Answer it,' came the call from the kitchen. Since Jaime, Isabel and Juan were for the moment absent, he was left to bemoan the fact that women expected men to do everything.

In the *entrada*, he lifted the receiver. 'Yes?'

'*Tempus fugit*, sweet Enrique.'

The line went dead.

'Who was it?' Dolores called out as he returned to the dining room.

'A wrong number.' He sat.

'Who did they want?'

'I've no idea.'

'They didn't say who they were?'

'No.'

She did not call him a liar, but he didn't doubt that was her opinion. Womanly intuition had named his caller a woman. Tempus fugit. The time before her husband was due to return from Paris? She had a cruel sense of humour, as witness her ambiguous conversation in the hearing of her husband, knowing he would understand little if anything. She would find it amusing to draw him to her house believing she was offering herself, and then reject him with the woman's cry that she was not that kind of a woman. When she was with a man, who was seducing whom? He would ignore her unspoken, erotic invitation. A woman who advised her availability was not to be trusted.

As he poured himself another drink, he congratulated himself on his common sense, self-control and will power.

He parked on the road above Ca Na Sophie, carefully made his way down the steep decline with a firm hold on the rope handrail. Sophie opened the door. Her dress was subtle; at first glance, it seemed it would reveal much, but didn't.

'You've had me worrying I might have lost any charm I once had,' she said.

'I've been very busy.'

'A man who prefers work to pleasure?'

'Pleasure has to wait.'

'Very sensible. The longer it is delayed, the more pleasurable it becomes. Do you intend just to stand there?'

He stepped into the hall.

'Marcel is in Paris and the disapproving maid has the day off, so I am on my own. Does that disturb you?'

'Why should it? Or will it boost your ego if I say I'm shaking all over?'

She laughed.

*   *   *

She began to twirl the hairs on his chest as they lay on the emperor-sized bed.

'Are you satisfied, dear inspector?'

'I suppose so.'

She pulled hard enough to dislodge a couple of hairs. 'No educated Frenchman could be so boorishly insulting.'

'I thought I was being generous.'

'Carry on like that and you can clear off.'

'Before the main course?'

'You've had your lot.'

He went to kiss her and she jerked her head away. He stroked her; when she tried to leave the bed, he pinned her down.

'I knew you'd act like a peasant,' she said.

'Then why invite me?' he asked, his head cushioned by her breasts.

'If you don't know, you're not very smart.'

'My superior believes me to be stupid. Certainly, I never have understood any woman.'

'So I have to explain you're here because you're so obviously a primitive, so unlike Charles?'

'Charles?'

'Charles Howes. So full of himself. Has to be told again and again how handsome, how refined he is.'

'What could you find in him to attract you?'

'I wanted to know what kind of a man he really is under that awful mask. And a missing wife always adds to the enjoyment. I suppose you want to know what he was like in bed?'

'No.'

'He might look a dream boy, but he had trouble.'

'Hardly surprising.'

'And now you wonder what his score was?'

'No.'

'Then I'll tell you. Four is being generous.'

'Do you always have an ulterior motive for entertaining someone?'

'Of course. Curiosity, a question mark, the fun of using a rod to play the fish.'

'What was it with Tyler?'

'So self-satisfied, so certain he could have what he wanted.'

'Which he did.'

'Until he discovered he began to need me a hell of a sight more than I needed him. Then I dropped him. It was quite amusing.'

'Who else have you bitched?'

'What a nasty way of putting it. And am I any crueller than you? You chase people and lock them up in jail. You offer pain; I provide pleasure. Sometimes it can be both. Which reminds me of poor Tim, although with him it was psychological pain, not physical.'

'Tim who?'

'Timothy Drew.'

'Impossible!'

'Don't be silly, sweetie. Where sex is concerned, nothing is impossible.'

'He and his wife are the closest of couples.'

'So he kept telling me as a sop to his conscience.'

'You snared him because he and his wife are so happy together? You're vicious.'

'And you're becoming boorishly nasty. Especially when there's no need to be upset. He was overcoming all his qualms when his bloody mobile went off.'

'When are you talking about?'

'God knows! I don't bother about days.'

'Think.'

'I won't.'

'Remember.'

'I won't.'

He moved his hands.

After a while, she said: 'I suppose it must have been the day people were in a state because Cyril had been shot. Can't think why. Everyone I knew thought it was rather amusing.'

'What was the time?'

'How would I know when he was shot?'

'The time when Drew was here.'

'Must have been in the morning because Marcel was returning in the afternoon and he's such a jealous husband.'

'Be more precise.'

'He thinks a man only has to talk to me to be working out how to get me to bed. Old men get more and more possessive as they become less and less capable.'

'Precise about the time.'

'I can't.'

'It's very important.'

'Not to me.'

He climbed off the bed.

'What are you going?'

'Work.'

'Don't be stupid.'

He crossed to the chair on which were his clothes.

'Please, sweet Enrique, don't go.'

He pulled his shirt over his shoulders.

'Come back and I promise to be as precise as I can be.'

He slowly discarded his shirt. As was written in the manual for serving officers in the Cuerpo, there was more than one way of gaining information.

NINETEEN

'Is there another piece of *coca*?' Alvarez asked.

Dolores turned around from the sink where she was washing plates, cups, saucers, glasses and cutlery. 'There is not the time for you to eat it since you did not come downstairs until I had called you three times.'

'It's Sunday.'

'Perhaps for you, but not for me. For me, it is just one more day when I have to cook many meals, wash and dry up, clear up the mess left by the rest of you, make certain the children are keeping out of mischief, and go shopping. If I spent Sundays as you suggest, the house would be dusty and there would be no food to put on the table.'

'You do work very hard.'

'A woman has no choice.'

'Few are as conscientious as you. I have been told that these days some women buy ready-made food from the supermarkets to avoid having to cook. Something you could not even consider doing.'

She finished cleaning a *plancha* and rested it on the draining board.

'I have to be off soon.'

'You should have left twenty minutes ago.'

'Salas will not be in his office. He'll be trying to play golf. So if there is another slice of *coca*? It's so good, you must have made it.'

'As my mother often had reason to say, praise holds even less substance than promise. What is left of the *coca* is in the cupboard.'

He did not move.

'You expect me to get it for you?'

He did, but thought it better not to say so. 'I'm not certain which cupboard.'

'On the right. The only certainty which the men of this house possess is whether there is enough wine and coñac.'

He stood, crossed to the cupboard, divided the remaining segment of *coca* in half, poured a second cup of coffee – since it seemed unlikely she would do that – and sat once more. He ate and drank slowly. There was so much to think about, so many questions to be answered.

'Are you not going to work?' she asked.

'What are you going to cook?' he asked from force of habit.

'*Sopas Mallorquinas.*'

One of those dishes which could be either reasonable or memorable, depending on the cook, the mixed grain bread, the freshness and quality of the cabbage stew. Since she was going to prepare the dish, it would be excellent . . . If only he were not faced by a problem which was not a problem.

Alvarez made his way up the stairs to his office. Eventually, he dialled Palma.

'I have been trying to contact you for the past half-hour,' the plum-voiced secretary said sharply.

'I had to drive down to the Port because of the report of a break-in.'

'Are you sending the details by fax or email?'

'It turned out the window was broken by kids playing football, not by someone forcing an entry, so that's hardly necessary.'

'You are still not aware that the superior chief has decreed every incident is to be reported, whether or not it has proved to be of any consequence?'

He vaguely remembered something like that. 'I will send in the report as soon as possible. Is Superior Chief Salas in his office?'

'Of course. He works every day of the week.'

Because he was careless of the well-being of his juniors. 'Can I speak to him?'

'Whether you may depends on what he is doing.'

Through the open window came the sounds of the market,

now so popular with tourists, many of whom were bussed
in from other parts of the island, that one had to visit it far
too early in the morning in order to buy the freshest vegetables, the sweetest almonds, the plumpest olives.

'I am informed, Alvarez, that I was unable to speak to
you earlier because you were investigating an incident in
the Port,' Salas said.

'Yes, señor.'

'And that you do not consider it necessary to make a
report of the incident despite my orders?'

His secretary had the nature of the school sneak. 'Only
unnecessary until I had spoken to you, señor.'

'You reported that Señor Drew has confessed the alibi
was false. Is that correct?'

'No, señor.'

'Why not?'

'He admits that he and the señora were not at Señor
Howes' villa at the relevant time.'

'Then his alibi was faked?'

'That is so.'

'Yet you have just denied that.'

'No, señor.'

'Dammit, you clearly said so.'

'I wasn't denying the faked alibi.'

'Have you the slightest idea what you are denying or
affirming?'

'Yes, señor.'

'I haven't.'

'He admits the alibi was faked, but he does have an alibi.'

'You are either under excessive mental strain, suffering
from that fall on your head when young, or are being inso-
lently stupid.'

'He has an alibi supported by another person.'

'Who?'

'Sophie Douste. The lady with blonde hair who has
appeared in this case more than once and is notably—'

'What was Drew doing with her?'

'That's difficult to say.'

'Because you have not bothered to find out?'

'He was in bed with her at the time of the murder. He could not present his true alibi because it would have shocked his wife.'

'I strongly doubt anything could shock such people.'

'Señor Drew has a warm, loving wife and they are the closest of couples.'

'You see no contradiction between your description of their relationship and the husband's behaviour?'

'It was just a brief temptation.'

'Which he lacked the strength of character to resist.'

'I doubt anyone could resist her.'

'An observation which slanders any man with morals. You realize the significance of this illicit relationship?'

'I think so.'

'If Drew did not shoot Tyler—'

'He admits he did.'

There was a brief silence.

'How typical, Alvarez, that you should not inform me of this fact before you had yet again indulged your fascination with matters of a carnal nature.'

'Unless I had spoken to Sophie, we would not have the information we now do.'

'Following his admission, you arrested Drew?'

'Not when he has an alibi for the time of Tyler's death which there is every reason to believe is genuine.'

'And if it is?'

'Then Señor Drew has made a false confession.'

'Have you bothered to ask yourself why he should do that?'

'He might be seeking notoriety or trying to make me look stupid.'

'Unnecessary.'

'There is a further possibility. He is trying to shield his wife.'

'It has taken you until now to understand the possibility of her guilt?'

'I naturally considered that from the beginning, but there was never reason to think it likely until I was certain Howes had been lying and neither husband nor wife had been with them. When I knew that, Señora Drew became a suspect. However, it became clear she could not be guilty.'

'Why not?'

'Higuero repeatedly said the driver of the car which caused him to fall over was a man, not a woman.'

'You see no error in what you have just said?'

'If a man was driving, he could not have been a woman.'

'Your error is in accepting Higuero's description of the driver when in our decadent era it is often difficult quickly to tell whether a figure is male or female.'

'He has always been very definite.'

'Since he is a Mallorquin, there is no reason to accept his evidence without doubting it. You will question him until he admits the obvious, that he could be wrong.'

'If I yet again query his judgement, he'll only become even more certain.'

'You lack the ability to carry out an efficient interrogation?'

'All I am trying to say—'

'Is of no account.'

It was the end of the call. Alvarez replaced the receiver. It was after midday. It was highly unlikely Higuero would be working at Es Teneres, so he could not be questioned until Monday which meant there was still a little of the weekend left to be enjoyed.

TWENTY

Higuero was sitting on a camp chair in the doorway of the garden shed. He watched Alvarez approach. 'What the hell is it this time?'

'Am I interrupting your work?'

'You trying to say I'm not entitled to a break when I'm exhausted? There's enough here to keep two overworked, but he expected me to have the place perfect on me own.' He stood, stepped down out of the shed.

'I won't interrupt your arduous work for long.'

'You won't interrupt it.' There was a pause. 'What's going to happen to me job?'

'Whoever buys the place will need someone. You can claim you are a gardener.'

'If you've nothing better to say, clear off.'

'I wish I could. Only I have to ask you about the day the señor was killed and you thought you were about to be run over by a car.'

'Thought? If I'd been your size, I'd be dead.'

'My superior chief has ordered me to come here and ask you a question.'

'Oh, he has, has he? What?'

'Who was driving the car?'

Higuero swore freely. 'Your boss must be as thick as you.'

'The evidence now suggests a woman might have been driving, not a man. You never saw the face, only the back of the head. In a state of shock, it would have been impossible to be certain of anything. Some women cut their hair short; some men let it grow long.'

Higuero reached down to break off a long stem of grass. He chewed the end of this for a while before he said: 'It happened so quick. It was only the back of the head . . .'

Alvarez was astonished and enraged. He had been certain

Higuero would never accept having been mistaken. Yet now it seemed as if he might be preparing to accept that was possible. If Drew's admission of guilt was proven to be false, it would be obvious he had lied to save his wife. Sandra would be accused of shooting a man who had earned the right to be shot. 'The superior chief spoke about charging you with giving false evidence. Unfortunately, he's a Madrileño and so refuses to believe what any of us Mallorquins say. Thinks we're all so stupid, we can't be trusted to tell the right time.'

'And he'll be so bleeding stupid he won't know where milk comes from.'

'Funny you should say that. Madrileños are so convinced they're always right and everyone else is wrong. I don't begin to get on with him. When I ask him to explain something, he tells me I'm as brainless as every other peasant on the island. He said one time that you probably didn't know who was driving the car because there were nothing but feathers between your ears.'

'You tell the stupid bastard it was a man.' Higuero stormed into the shed, his expression one of unyielding stubbornness.

There would be no change of evidence, Alvarez thought as he walked back to his car. He sat behind the wheel. Common sense said he was a fool to have deliberately goaded Higuero into refusing to admit error.

Because of the evidence Sophie had provided, because of the false confession, it seemed very likely Sandra Drew had been driving. He started the engine, did not immediately drive off. There was just the chance Sophie had been maliciously lying, her perverse character finding it amusing to do so.

The bedroom was cool, thanks to the air-conditioning unit set to a low temperature. On each bedside table was a filled glass – Veuve Clicquot in hers, Fundador on ice in his. They enjoyed the relaxation which came from satiation.

He was the first to speak. 'I have to ask you something.'

'Ten.'

'To do with work.'

'What an utter boor you can be.'

'Did you tell me the truth when you said Drew had been here on the day Tyler was shot?'

'Why should I have lied?'

'Because it would have amused you.'

'I gain my amusement in other ways.'

'Were you lying?'

'No.'

'You swear you weren't?'

'I'll swear if you go on like this.'

'It's vitally important for someone I know the truth.'

'I'm not interested in your someone.'

'Drew was here that Thursday?'

'Yes, yes, yes. Ask again and I'll say he bloody wasn't.'

'What happened?'

'He came here, as nervous as a kid of fifteen used to be when you were young. Wanted a drink, took time drinking it. I told him, if he was like that, take his conscience back to his wife and don't play at being a grown man. In the end, he started undressing . . . I've told you that.'

'Tell me again.'

'His mobile rang. And he answered it!'

'People have different priorities.'

'The next thing, he's shouting into the phone he'll go there and look for something. He dressed and ran out.' She giggled. 'They say there's always a first time.'

He climbed off the bed.

'If you think you're going to make it a second time . . .'

'I need to think and can't do that next to you.'

'What the hell d'you mean?'

'I'll return when I've done the thinking.'

'Clear off now and I'll goddamn well lock you out!'

'I'll take the keys with me.'

'You think I'll have anything more to do with a selfish peasant?'

'Annoyed you haven't been able to reduce me to servitude?'

'Annoyed I was ever stupid enough to have anything to do with you.'

He dressed, left the house and sat in his car. How could the phone call Drew had received have been so explosively important that he had left her bed? He had shouted over the mobile that he'd go there and look for it. Es Teneres? The gun which had killed Tyler, fired by Sandra? He had not known that very few revolvers or automatics, with their pimpled stocks and narrow triggers, provided worthwhile prints. When his wife had phoned as he was about to betray her with another woman and said she had shot Tyler, it was small wonder he had left in a wild hurry.

Alvarez's mind returned to the past. Sandra, convinced even a man like Tyler would finally respond to the request of a grieving mother, had returned to Es Teneres on her own, knowing her husband would have vetoed another visit. The cook was ill, Julia was trying to prepare a meal so she was unobserved.

Tyler would have been contemptuously dismissive. Two people had been rundown and killed? Hundreds of people were killed on the roads every year. It was a fact of death. And if a couple walked in the middle of a country lane, arms about each other, careless of other users of the road, they were asking for trouble.

Her grief had been exacerbated by his verbal cruelty. She temporarily lost all self-control. She frightened him with the strength of her fury. He had become alarmed, had brought the automatic out of a drawer in the desk to protect himself. His obvious cowardice had the effect of calming her down – he was even more contemptuous than she had thought. Noting her returned self-control, ashamed of his weakness, he had taunted her. If she was so mistakenly certain he had killed her daughter, would it help her to kill him? . . . If he wronged her, should she not revenge? . . . He would lay the gun down on the desk and she could use it. That was unless she lacked the courage to do anything but shout ridiculous nonsense . . .

Her violet emotions had been re-engaged. Now beyond coherent thought, she had gone forward and picked up the gun. Not just frightened, but terrified, he had struggled to take it from her. In the struggle the gun had gone off. Or perhaps there had been no struggle. A strong-willed woman . . .

Alvarez accepted he would never know the truth. Thankfully, there was no need to. Higuero would have to be asked yet again how certain he was that the driver of the car was male. There could now be no fear he would suffer uncertainty. The driver would be male. Which, ironically, was the truth.

Following the call on the mobile, terrified by what his wife had told him, Drew had rushed to Es Teneres to rescue the gun, fearful her prints would incriminate her. What had saved them both had been the temperature of the library, too cold to allow even a reasonable time of death to be given so that small inconsistencies of time had been ignored.

Salas would truthfully be told there could be no further question regarding the sex of the driver. Since Drew had a solid alibi, the driver had not been he. In such circumstances, the only logical possibility was Tyler had been shot by an aggrieved husband. Unless and until that husband could be named, the killer would not be identified.

Alvarez left the car, returned to the house, went upstairs. The bedroom had not been locked.